G.J. KEMP

THE ACRE SERIES

Petra and the Sewer Rats
(A Juno and the Lady Novella Book 1.2)

for Alphie

ACKNOWLEDGMENTS

To my incredible team who have helped get this novella out. Jess and Isabelle, for your guidance. My beta readers, Nanna and Lara. My editors, Claire from Cherry Edits and Andy from The Narrative Craft. Andrei for your wonderful cover. Latifa (@latifahdesign) for all your design work. And Ashley for all your hard work on my socials.

Thank you.

THE ACRE SERIES

Thank you for your interest in The Acre Series. I recommend you read the principal novels in order as the characters and the story grow with the series. The novellas are prequels and sequels to the principal novels. You can read them in any order you wish.

—

The Acre Series
Principal Books
Juno and the Lady (An Acre Story Book 1)

Miles and the Soldier (An Acre Story Book 2)

Juno and the Lady Novellas
Valen and the Beasts: A Juno and the Lady Novella (An Acre Story Book 1.1)

Petra and the Sewer Rats: A Juno and the Lady Novella (An Acre Story Book 1.2)

CHAPTER I
GIRL STUFF

'Nat,' Petra said, throwing her hand up over her mouth. 'For how long?'

A grin stretched across Nat's face. 'I have known Peter for a long time, so it was bound to happen.'

'Are you going to stay with him?' Petra said. 'His new role as captain will give him good status.'

Nat shook her head. 'Leonard has chosen me to be his wife. I must do as I am told to bring honour to my family. You know the rules.'

Petra scrunched up her nose. 'Leonard isn't very good-looking, is he?'

Nat jabbed her chin over at Peter, then let out a dramatic sigh. 'Compared to that beautiful man, he is definitely not good-looking.'

'How many times have you been with him?' Petra said, a sly look spreading across her face.

With a small shrug, Nat winked at Petra.

'You are so bad,' Petra said.

'It is not illegal,' Nat said. 'I am not married yet.'

'But what about Leonard?' Petra said. 'Does he suspect?'

Nat shook her head. 'I will tell him when the time is right.'

'Leonard is the right choice, though,' Petra said. 'The people of Fairacre respect him highly. You will do your family proud.'

'Yes,' Nat said, lowering herself onto the bench next to Petra. 'I am going to break it off with Peter in the next few days. I don't want Leonard to change his mind.'

'And I don't want you to be maid to my family for the rest of your life,' Petra said. 'So don't mess it up, you hear?'

Nat looked up and bit her bottom lip. 'I need to speak to your father about that.'

Petra lifted an eyebrow. 'What do you mean? Is there something wrong?'

'No, no,' Nat said. 'I will ask if I can still look after his household even after I marry Leonard.'

'Why on earth would you want to do that?' Petra said. 'I don't think Leonard would allow it, would he?'

'Leonard will allow it,' Nat said. 'He is totally in love with me and all he wants to do is make me happy. If he doesn't allow it, I will make his life hell.'

'Oh, I have no doubt,' Petra said, letting out a long sigh. 'You are so lucky you have someone who loves you that much.'

'Do you think your father will allow me to continue working here?' Nat said.

'My father will allow it,' Petra said. 'Or I will make his life hell otherwise.'

They both laughed out loud.

'What is going on over there?' Peter said, lifting his glass. 'Myself and Hargreaves are keeping an eye on you two.'

Petra waved him away. 'Girl stuff. You wouldn't understand.'

Peter filled his cheeks with air and blew out a long breath. Hargreaves snorted, then raised his glass in the girl's direction.

Petra turned to Nat. 'I will speak to my father on his return. I am sure he will be OK with it. Since Mama passed, it's just been the two of us, and he knows how much I care for you.'

'It would be lonely without me here,' Nat said, smiling sweetly.

'Well, I still have Harold, you know, so, whatever,' Petra said with a shrug.

'Hey,' Nat said, playfully punching Petra's shoulder.

Petra chuckled. 'You have been my best friend ever since I can remember.'

Nat looked up at the crystal-clear blue sky. 'Everything is going to change soon, isn't it?'

'It is, but at least we will still be in the same town,' Petra said, lifting her head and closing her eyes as the afternoon sun kissed her face.

The stone feature in the middle of the garden gargled as water splashed into the pond. A massive bumblebee buzzed in front of Petra, then shot to the flower bed.

'Nasty things,' Petra said, waving her hand in front of her face.

'Do you know when your father will be back?' Nat said, turning her gaze onto Peter.

'Stop staring, Nat,' Petra said as she waved Harold over.

'Yes, my lady,' Harold said, with a slight bow.

'Is my father still coming home tonight?'

'He will be here when the sun disappears over the horizon,' Harold said.

'Thank you, Harold,' Petra said, passing him an empty glass.

Harold bowed, then made his way to Peter and Hargreaves.

'Are you going to tell him when he gets back?' Nat said, still staring at Peter.

'Tell him what?' Petra said, raising her eyebrow.

'Oh, come on,' Nat said, looking back at Petra and throwing

her hands up in the air. 'You know exactly what I am talking about.'

Petra shook her head. 'I do not know what you mean.'

'You and Hargreaves!' Nat said, slightly too loudly.

Petra's mouth dropped open. 'How do you know about him?'

Nat doubled over as her whole body shook with laughter.

'How did you know?' Petra whispered. 'I was so careful.'

'I have known you most of my life,' Nat said, wiping a tear from her eye. 'Did you honestly think you could keep this from me?'

'Yes, I thought I could,' Petra said, still whispering. 'I was hoping nobody would find out.'

'Your secret is safe with me,' Nat said, wrapping her arms around Petra and giving her a squeeze. 'Just don't be too hard on me and Peter.'

Petra gave her best friend a squeeze. 'I won't.'

'What is going on?' Hargreaves said, walking over with Peter.

Nat cleared her throat and wiped another tear off her cheek. 'We were talking about Petra's father. He should be home shortly.'

'Is that really what you two were talking about?' Hargreaves said, with a quick glance at Petra.

'Yes, it was,' Nat said, trying to kick Hargreaves in the shin. 'Behave yourself.'

Peter offered his hand and pulled Nat to her feet. 'You have told her, haven't you?'

Nat looked at Petra. Petra snorted, and then they both burst out laughing.

Hargreaves raised his head to the sky. Peter rolled his eyes and shook his head.

'My lady,' Harold called from the back door. 'Guest traders are waiting in the trades room.'

Hargreaves offered Petra his hand.

Petra took Hargreaves's outstretched hand and pulled herself to her feet. 'Thank you, Harold. I trust you have served them the standard drinks.'

'Yes, my lady,' Harold said. 'They always enjoy the fine wine your father has on offer.'

'Our exalted lady needs to go to work,' Peter said with a wave and a bow.

'Behave yourself, young captain,' Petra said, walking down to the house. 'I will be back soon.'

'My lady,' Harold said, holding the door open.

Petra smiled at Harold. She lifted her dress up from the floor, held it in position, and then strode off to the trades room. At the double doors, she stopped, breathed deeply, let go of her dress, and pulled herself up to her full height. The doors swung open. 'Good afternoon, gentlemen,' she said, striding into the room. 'It is very good to see you.'

The hard lines on the tradesmen's faces softened as Petra walked over. They bowed their heads as she shook their hands one by one, before taking a seat.

'It is good to see you, my lady,' a tradesman said.

'Please, sit,' Petra said, waving a hand at the chairs opposite the large oak desk. 'What is it I can do for you?'

'If I may be so bold, my lady,' a tradesman said, pulling his cap off his head. 'The City of Lynn has been complaining about the quality of clothes coming from Fairacre. They say our standards have dropped.'

Petra's face hardened. 'And to this, what do you say, sir?'

Another tradesman cleared his throat. 'I think our standards are dropping, my lady. But this is because the quality of materials has been declining.'

'And you, sir?' Petra said, moving her eyes to the next tradesman.

'I agree, my lady. The quality of the trimming materials has been in steady decline for months.'

Petra gave the trader a nod, then turned to the next. 'Your thoughts, sir?'

'If we want, we at Fairacre can create the trimmings ourselves, my lady,' the tradesman said. 'But this may affect our trade relationship with the City of Lynn.'

'What would your solution be, sir?' Petra said, looking at the final, older tradesman.

'We only wish you or your father would complain about the trimmings and their average quality.'

Petra tapped her nails against the desk. After a few moments, she stood. 'Leave this with me, gentlemen. I shall request that the weavers create a set of trimmings. When the time is right, I will have you send word to your suppliers that we will create our own material and trimmings. That will focus the minds of the trimmers in the City of Lynn.'

The tradesmen all rose together. 'A wise decision, my lady,' one said. 'Please give my regards to your father.'

Petra inclined her head once. 'I will give my regards. Harold, we are done.'

'Yes, my lady,' Harold said, appearing out of nowhere.

'Can you see our tradesmen out?' Petra said, walking around the oak desk.

Harold held open the trades room doors and signalled for the men to leave.

The second-to-last tradesman stopped halfway through the doors and looked up at Harold. 'A man working for a woman,' he said, snarling. 'Have you no respect?'

'This is Ernest's house. It would be wise to keep your mouth shut,' another tradesman said.

'He works for my father,' Petra said, walking up to Harold.

'And my words are my father's words. Would you like me to pass your complaint through to my father?'

The tradesman turned with wide eyes. 'No, no, my lady. Please accept my deepest apologies.'

Petra gave the trader a single nod.

'This way, please,' Harold said, extending a hand to show the way to the front door.

Petra watched the men walk into the street. A tight-lipped smile spread across her face as the whispers of the men cursing each other filtered through the doorway. With her fluffy dress pulled up off her ankles, Petra walked out of the trades room and returned to the back garden.

'Everything OK?' Peter said, with a concerned look.

'There is something going on in the City of Lynn,' Petra said. 'The quality of the material we are receiving from them is declining.'

'That is very unusual,' Nat said. 'They usually send us their best, do they not?'

'Yes, they do,' Petra said, tapping her chin with her finger.

'They are also reducing their orders of our finest clothes,' Hargreaves said. 'However, food orders have been increasing.'

'We will speak to Papa when he gets home. He will know what is going on,' Petra said. 'Will the two of you stay for dinner?'

Hargreaves and Peter bowed at Petra. 'It would be an honour, my lady.'

'Excellent,' Petra said. 'For now, we will have a small snack. Harold, can you get us cold meats?'

'Yes, my lady,' Harold said.

They chatted among themselves as Harold delivered small trays of meat to the table. The sun began its long journey to the western horizon. The faint giggles of children filtered into the garden.

'These are fantastic, Harold,' Hargreaves said as he shoved another slice of ham into his mouth.

Harold's neck turned a slight tinge of pink. 'Thank you, sir. It comes from the market in the south of Fairacre.'

Petra dabbed her mouth with a napkin. 'I have only visited the market once.'

Nat, Hargreaves and Peter stared at Petra with their mouths open.

'What?' Petra said, shrugging her shoulders.

'You have only ever been to the market once?' Peter said. 'Fairacre's market, which is down the north–south road?'

'Well, yes,' Petra said. 'There is no reason for me to go. Everything is here for me in the northern district and in the entertainment district.'

'That makes sense, my lady,' Harold said, with a warning glance at Peter and Hargreaves.

'Fairacre is not that big,' Nat said, shaking her head. 'I thought you would know it all.'

Petra pursed her lips. 'I know more about the City of Lynn than I do about Fairacre.'

Nat sat forward. 'You promised us you would describe the City of Lynn one day.'

'I will,' Petra said. 'It has been a few seasons since I was there last though, so things may have changed.'

'I would so love to visit that magnificent city,' Nat said. 'It would beat doing your father's laundry every day.'

'A good afternoon to everyone.'

Nat dropped her glass with a crash.

'Papa,' Petra said, spinning around. 'You are back.'

'That I am,' Ernest said. 'How are you? How is everyone?'

Petra skipped to her father and threw her arms around his neck. 'You were gone too long this time, Papa.'

Ernest closed his eyes as he hugged his daughter. 'I am sorry, my dear. I needed to take care of a lot of business.'

'Sir,' Harold said, bowing low.

'I am sorry for what I said, sir,' Nat said, picking up pieces of the shattered glass.

The corners of Ernest's mouth turned upwards. 'Is my laundry that bad, Natalie?'

Nat chuckled. 'Absolutely not, sir.'

'How are you both?' Ernest said, pointing his chin at Peter and Hargreaves.

'Very well, sir,' Peter replied, with a bow.

'All the better for seeing you, sir,' Hargreaves said, also bowing.

'Such a perfect gentleman,' Ernest said. 'I trust you are behaving yourselves in my house?'

'I have asked them to stay for dinner, Papa,' Petra said, quickly stepping in.

'A splendid idea. Any business to take care of?'

Petra's face turned serious. 'I have news from the tradesmen.'

'Am I to assume you have taken care of everything?'

'Of course, Papa,' Petra said.

'A brilliant businesswoman she is, sir,' Hargreaves said.

A look of sadness spread across Ernest's face. 'We all know she is not allowed to be a businesswoman in Fairacre, Hargreaves. It is the rules.'

'Yes, sir,' Hargreaves said, looking away. 'It is very unfortunate, sir.'

'And how are you, Natalie?' Ernest said. 'Your wedding is not long now, is it?'

Nat's cheeks turned pink. 'Yes, sir. If everything goes according to plan, Leonard and I will be married in the spring.'

'A good man that Leonard is,' Ernest said. 'Do nothing silly to mess it up now, Natalie.'

Nat's mouth hung open. Peter choked, then coughed loudly. Ernest raised an eyebrow at Peter.

'He knows you too well, Nat,' Petra said, smirking. 'You must learn to behave.'

Nat's mouth slammed shut. 'Yes, my lady,' she said, clearing her throat. 'Please excuse me, I need to unpack your father's things.'

Ernest chuckled as Nat skipped past him.

'I am going to freshen up,' Petra said. 'Harold, can you take the boys through to the dining room?'

'Yes, my lady,' Harold said.

Petra strode down the garden path and through the back doors.

An hour later, Petra, Hargreaves, Peter and Ernest sat at the thick oak dining room table. Harold strode in with a silver tray filled with meats and vegetables. Nat circled the table, making sure all glasses were full.

'I would like the two of you to join us,' Petra said, signalling to Harold and Nat.

'I beg your pardon, my lady?' Harold said.

'You heard her, Harold,' Ernest said. 'Both of you pull up a chair and sit. You are part of this family.'

The two servants looked at each other. Nat pulled a chair out from underneath the table. She cleared her throat, then sat and waited for Harold to push her chair in. Harold walked around the table and sat opposite Nat.

'Tell us about the City of Lynn, Papa,' Petra said. 'Are there changes happening?'

Ernest's face darkened. 'Change is indeed happening. I sense dark days ahead. But first, you must tell me of the traders, as I feel somehow the stories are connected.'

'There are complaints our product is not of the highest quality,' Petra said. 'The trimmings are not up to standard.'

'What did you suggest?' Ernest said, his forehead crinkling.

'I have instructed our weavers to create trimmings using our own material.'

'Is it not the fault of the material, though?' Peter said, nervously glancing at Ernest. 'How is creating our own trimmings with poor material a good idea?'

Ernest spread his hands. 'Well, my love?'

'The material is of lower quality. But showing the City of Lynn we can use our own material to make our own trimmings may cause them to re-evaluate the quality of what they send us,' Petra said. 'Why purchase material from the City of Lynn when we can use our own?'

'Exactly,' Ernest said, clapping his hands together. 'Did the traders accept your decision?'

'I have told them to use it as a tool to threaten their suppliers,' Petra said. 'And I have also said that if it doesn't work, we will source better material and continue making our own.'

Ernest nodded his head slowly. 'A wise decision, Petra. They either supply us with correct material for the trimming, or we source our own to maintain a high-quality product.'

'I remember you saying that quality is everything, Papa,' Petra said. 'Without it, the nobles of the City of Lynn would not buy our product.'

'That is correct,' Ernest said. 'Quality will always beat quantity. Make a superior product and people will buy it.'

'Just like this meal,' Hargreaves said, raising a glass at Harold.

'Thank you, sir,' Harold said.

'You're a genius when it comes to food,' Petra said, smiling fondly at him.

'I wish to return to my duties now, sir,' Harold said, clearing his throat.

Ernest smiled at the old man. 'Of course.'

Nat stood at the same time as Harold. They continued working the table, making sure everyone had food and drink.

Through the rest of the evening, they sat at the dining table and spoke of the City of Lynn and Fairacre. Half an hour before midnight, Hargreaves and Peter wished Petra and Ernest good-night. Petra and Nat closed the front door behind the young men.

'I have further news for you,' Ernest said to Petra as she returned to the dining room. 'Will you join me?'

'Of course,' Petra said, following her father through the house and into his study.

'I think I have found you a suitor.'

Petra's eyebrows shot up. 'Who is he?' she said, sitting forward.

'His name is Donte,' Ernest said. 'He has a chain of shops in the City of Lynn.'

'What shops, Father,' Petra said.

'He specialises in materials for clothes,' Ernest said with a smirk. 'It seems we need to speak to him about the quality of his material, don't we?'

'He does not sound very honourable, Father,' Petra said.

Ernest bit his bottom lip. 'I will have a word with him.'

'Does that mean I have to move to the City of Lynn?' Petra said.

'No,' Ernest said. 'He has a business here in Fairacre. His staff keep our town clean. He wants to move out of the city and come to live in Fairacre.'

'And he is a noble?' Petra said.

'That he is, my dear,' Ernest said.

Petra clapped her hands. 'Finally, Father. If I marry this Donte, we may move our family into the higher classes of society.'

Ernest sat back and steepled his fingers. 'What of Hargreaves?'

The whole of Petra's world spun in front of her. 'What do you mean?'

'Steady, my love,' Ernest said, leaning forward and grabbing her hand. 'I have known of your relationship with Hargreaves for some time.'

Petra licked her dry lips. 'I am sorry, Papa. I did not wish for you to find out. Have I dishonoured our family?'

'You are not married,' Ernest said. 'You can do as you please, just don't advertise it.'

With a sigh of relief, Petra relaxed into her chair.

'I can see sadness on your face,' Ernest said. 'Do you love Hargreaves?'

'I don't know, Papa,' Petra said, looking down at her hands. 'It doesn't matter, anyway. Donte sounds like the perfect man to help advance our family.'

Ernest sat back and let out a long sigh. 'It will pain me if you are not happy.'

'Was Mother happy when you chose her?' Petra said.

'Ha,' Ernest said, with a snort. 'She could not stand me. She said I was a pompous man-child with too much money.'

Petra placed a hand over her mouth and giggled.

'It took me a few seasons to win her over,' Ernest said, grinning. 'She was definitely worth it, though. I found her to be the most beautiful woman in the world.'

'She loved you more than anything,' Petra said. 'I will learn to love Donte if that is what I must do. When will he be here in Fairacre?'

'Before the boldness of summer hits us,' Ernest said. 'In about a week or two.'

'I will make the preparations,' Petra said. 'And I will have to tell Hargreaves that it is over between us.'

'I have some news about Hargreaves,' Ernest said.

'Oh?' Petra said. 'He is not in any trouble, is he, Father?'

'No, my love, quite the opposite. We have decided he will be the new mayor of Fairacre.'

Petra's mouth fell open. 'His application was successful?'

'It was,' Ernest said. 'With some obvious influencing on my part. He is very capable and will do our town proud.'

'He will be so pleased, Papa,' Petra said.

Ernest nodded. 'Yes, I think he will be.'

A quiet knock sounded from the study door.

'Come,' Ernest said, looking up.

'Your late-night snack, sir,' Harold said, then walked into the study with a tray. 'May I get something for you, my lady?'

'I am OK, thanks, Harold,' Petra said.

'My lady,' Harold said as he gave a small bow.

Petra watched him walk out of the study, then she turned to her father. 'I need to ask a question, Papa.'

'Yes?' Ernest said, while sniffing the foul-smelling snack that Harold had left.

'Why does Harold serve me? I am a woman.'

Ernest dumped the snack back on the plate. 'He is your grandfather.'

Petra coughed and spluttered. 'He is what?'

'Are you OK?' Ernest said, leaning forward and slapping Petra hard on her back.

'He is my grandfather?' Petra said, gasping and wheezing for air.

'He sacrificed himself to make sure his daughter married well,' Ernest said. 'He chose to be my servant for the rest of his life as long as I married your mother.'

Petra stared. 'He is my grandfather?'

'You already asked me that, my dear,' Ernest said with a smile.

'Why didn't you tell me?' Petra said, her voice lowering in anger.

'For his and your mother's protection,' Ernest said, as he twirled his glass. 'We couldn't have a young girl telling everyone that her grandfather is her servant. It would have drawn the worst kind of attention to our family.'

'Who else knows?' Petra said.

'Nobody,' Ernest said. 'And that is the way it needs to stay, Petra. If the men of this town find out, they will end Harold's life.'

'That is so unfair,' Petra said, grinding her teeth.

'It is the way of our world,' Ernest said. 'Life is never fair.'

'May I tell him I know?' Petra said.

Ernest gave his daughter a knowing grin. 'No point asking me. You are going to tell him, anyway.'

Petra chuckled. 'You do know me well, Papa. I will tell him in the morning.'

'Remember, it will be a shock to him,' Ernest said. 'I don't think he ever expected me to tell you any of this.'

'I will be gentle. So, tell me more about your trip.'

A cloud descended over Ernest's face. He propped his head back on the chair's headrest.

'What is it, Papa?' Petra said, sitting forward.

'There is news of war,' Ernest said. 'An unknown force from the north is descending into our lands.'

'Is this true, or just gossip?' Petra said. 'We know how City people love their gossip.'

'The City is in crisis,' Ernest said. 'A man named Dr Viktor is frantically building massive steel machines.'

A confused frown spread over Petra's forehead. 'Steel machines? What is a machine?'

'Great enormous metal beasts that throw clouds of black smoke into the air,' Ernest said. 'Rumour has it we need the machines to defend ourselves.'

Petra leant further forward. 'What do they look like?'

Ernest rubbed his chin. 'I don't know, daughter. They did not allow me into the northern district. All I could see were the clouds of smoke they create.'

'They didn't let you into parts of the city?' Petra said, with a look of shock. 'You have a key to the city. Aren't you allowed access to the entire city?'

'The key has its limits,' Ernest said, patting the key that hung from his neck. 'Dr Viktor did not allow me to enter.'

'Who is this Dr Viktor?' Petra said.

'He is a funny old man with a cane and an awful cough. He walks around shouting orders all day. It seems he is the architect of these impressive metal beasts.'

'Can I come with you when you visit again?' Petra said, her eyes brightening. 'I am sure I can get us into the northern district to see these machines.'

'Meet Donte first. We can plan once we sort things out with him.'

'Yes, Papa,' Petra said.

'I have finished my evening drink and I think I will retire. I have not rested since travelling,' Ernest said.

'Of course, Papa,' Petra said. 'How silly of me! Please go to sleep and I will see you in the morning.'

Ernest struggled out of the chair, then walked over to the study door. As he opened the door, he looked back at his daughter. 'End it with Hargreaves, Petra. I will not be best pleased if Donte finds out and refuses to marry you.'

'Yes, Papa,' Petra said. 'I shall do this immediately.'

'Goodnight, my love.'

'Night, Papa,' Petra said.

The door clicked shut. Petra let out a long breath, then fell back into the oversized chair.

After a few minutes, a gentle knock sounded on the study door.

'Who's there?' Petra hissed.

'It is only me,' Nat said, her head appearing around the door. 'Oh my, what is wrong?'

'He knows,' Petra said, a lump forming in her throat. 'He knows about Hargreaves.'

Nat closed the door behind her. 'What did he say? Was he angry?'

Petra shook his head. 'No, he was OK with it.'

'Then why the tears?' Nat said, a frown forming.

Petra placed her hand on her belly.

'Oh no,' Nat said. 'Oh no, no, no. You cannot be pregnant, Petra.'

'I am not sure yet,' Petra said.

'How could you be so stupid?' Nat hissed.

'I wasn't thinking,' Petra said, her voice trembling.

'Hargreaves is just as stupid,' Nat growled as she paced the study. 'How many days are you late?'

'Just two,' Petra said.

Nat stopped and rolled her eyes at Petra. 'It is early to say you are with child, Petra. Let's see what happens over the next few days?'

'What happens if I am with child, though?' Petra said. 'It will ruin everything.'

'Let us deal with that when the time comes,' Nat said. 'The Fairacre doctor will have some remedies, I am sure.'

Petra placed her other hand on her belly. 'I pray there is nothing in here. My family has worked so hard to become nobles. It would ruin everything.'

Nat sat, then laid her head on Petra's lap. 'We will sort something out. Don't worry about it.'

'And another thing,' Petra said, stroking Nat's hair. 'Harold is my grandfather.'

Nat snorted, then broke out into a coughing fit. 'You what?' she said, sitting up.

'Keep it down,' Petra said, waving her hand. 'You will wake Papa.'

'What do you mean, Harold is your grandfather?' Nat said.

'It was a condition my father set,' Petra said. 'He would marry my mother if her father agreed to a life of service.'

'Why did he do that?' Nat said.

'I have no idea,' Petra said. 'I will ask him tomorrow.'

Nat laid her head back in Petra's lap. 'I think it would be best if I was there when you speak to him. Harold will feel exposed.'

'Yes, I think that is a good idea,' Petra said. 'Can I ask a favour, please?'

With her eyes closed, Nat hummed a response.

'Can you take me on a tour of Fairacre tomorrow? I think it would be a good idea for me to get to know the town I was born in.'

'Are you sure? There are a lot of things out there you might not like,' Nat said. 'It can be quite dangerous for a northern district girl.'

'I am sure,' Petra said. 'Before I marry Donte, I want to know as much as I can. I want to make sure he feels welcome in our town.'

'Well, that is a deal then,' Nat said. 'We can leave straight after breakfast if your father is OK with it.'

'He will agree,' Petra said. 'I think it has always annoyed him that I know little about our town. Especially since most of our business is in the weaving district.'

Nat sat up then stood. 'Well then, my lady. I suggest you turn in. It will be a long day tomorrow.'

Petra grabbed Nat's outstretched hand and pulled herself up. 'Can you make sure my walking shoes are in order?'

'I will lay everything out for you, my lady,' Nat said. 'Make sure you get some good rest.'

'Goodnight, Nat,' Petra said, walking over to the study doors. 'And remember: tell nobody of our conversation.'

'Of course, my lady,' Nat said with a bow.

Petra walked out of the study and up the centre staircase to the second floor. She strode down the corridor to the double doors that opened into her living quarters. With a click, the doors closed behind her.

CHAPTER 2
THE WEAVING DISTRICT

'I have been waiting at the front door for fifteen minutes,' Nat said. 'You are always late.'

'Yes, yes,' Petra said, double-stepping down the stairs. 'I couldn't get into these shoes. Are you sure these are the right ones?'

Nat held the front door open. 'They are the only ones.'

'Where is Harold?' Petra said. 'I didn't see him at breakfast this morning.'

'I don't know,' Nat said, shrugging. 'Probably doing something for your papa.'

'Do you think my papa told him about me knowing?' Petra said, biting her bottom lip.

'I don't think your papa would take that away from you,' Nat said, waving her hand through the door. 'Come on, let's get going.'

Petra glanced one more time around the house, then stepped out into the brilliant morning sunshine. The door banged behind her, making her jump.

'Sorry,' Nat said, taking her by the arm. 'Are you ready for our adventure?'

'I am,' Petra said, grinning at her best friend. 'I want to see as much as possible.'

They searched for shade by walking under the trees that lined the wide cobblestone road.

'My lady,' a passing man said as he gave a deep bow. 'Good day to you and your father. Say hello to him, would you?'

Petra inclined her head. 'I will.'

Five more steps and another man bowed. 'My lady. I hope you and your father are doing well.'

'This is going to get tiring,' Nat said. 'I should cover your head, so nobody knows who you are.'

'Oh shush,' Petra said, squeezing Nat's hand. 'I will make sure we don't chat with everyone.'

A few minutes later, they reached the end of the road. Both stopped and stared at the town of Fairacre that lay below them. The flat roofs stretched across the east, west and south of the town. Only in the north of Fairacre stood the large mansions with angled rooftops.

'Where should we go first?' Petra said.

'I think we should stop at the town square first,' Nat said.

'And then the market in the south,' Petra said. 'Harold always goes to the market and I want to see why he loves it so much.'

'Then the market it is,' Nat said, propelling them both forward. 'Watch your step now. This road really gets steep.'

They continued down the winding road, with Petra saying good morning to every person who acknowledged her. The road flattened as the trees on the path disappeared. The town hall loomed high above them.

'What is that place?' Petra said, pointing to a set of steps that went underneath the town hall.

'The jail,' Nat said. 'Many women have been unlucky enough to visit that hellhole.'

'If they misbehave, then we should put them in jail,' Petra said with a single nod. 'It's why it is there.'

Nat mumbled under her breath.

'What?' Petra said, looking at her friend.

'Sometimes they send women to jail for nothing more than stealing a piece of food, my lady,' Nat said. 'Fairacre is not how you imagine it.'

Petra opened her mouth to speak.

'Oh look, it's Hargreaves and Peter,' Nat said, interrupting and waving at the two men.

Peter, the young captain, grinned and waved back. Hargreaves gave them both a small bow.

The two women wove through the busy town square until they reached them.

'Good morning,' Hargreaves said. 'I cannot stay for long as your father is in the town hall.'

'Oh,' Petra said, her face dropping. 'I was hoping we could spend some time together.'

'I am afraid your father comes first,' Hargreaves said with a look of sadness. 'Will you stop in on your way home this afternoon?'

Petra smiled. 'Of course.'

'See, that's how it should be,' a boy said, appearing next to Peter. 'A woman doing what she is told.'

'Exactly right,' another boy said, appearing on Peter's other side.

Peter grabbed both boys by the collar and bashed their heads together.

The boys grabbed the sides of their heads and rubbed hard.

'Dec, Jon, this is Petra, Ernest's daughter,' Hargreaves said.

Both Jon and Dec forgot their sore heads and turned with eyes like saucers to stare at Petra. 'Sorry, my lady, I never knew,' Dec said. 'Sorry, my lady,' Jon mumbled under his breath.

'Don't worry, my lady,' Peter said, grinning. 'I will soon have these young soldiers sorted out.'

Nat chuckled at Peter. 'The captain of Fairacre, my knight in shining armour.'

Peter waggled his eyebrows at Nat, then looked over at Petra. 'Are you ready for your Fairacre adventure?'

'We are,' Petra said, clapping her hands together. 'First, the market, then I would like to explore the weaving district.'

'The weaving district?' Peter said, frowning. 'Are you sure you want to go down there? It is best to stick to the shops on the east–west road.'

'I would like to explore the whole town, Peter,' Petra said, folding her arms.

Peter gave Petra a small bow. 'If you wish, but please, let me give you a couple of guards for protection.'

'I will protect them,' a woman said. 'Ain't nothing getting in my way in the weaving district.'

Petra turned and raised an eyebrow at the young woman, who stood with a hand on one hip.

'Greta, get out of here,' Peter said. 'Go on. Get back to where you belong.'

Greta pulled a tongue at Peter, then made down the southern road.

'Who is that?' Petra said.

'Works in the entertainment district,' Peter said. 'Serves drinks in the bars.'

'We should be fine in the weaving district,' Nat said. 'We are only going a little way in.'

Peter bit his bottom lip. 'Stay away from the alleys. And here, take this whistle. Blow on it if you need help.'

Nat took the whistle and hung it from her neck. She turned to Petra. 'My lady. Shall we proceed?'

'My lady this, my lady that,' Peter said, poking Nat in the ribs.

Petra took Nat's arm and walked towards the southern road. 'Ignore him. We have a town to explore.'

As they wove through the town square and onto the north–south road, men who recognised Petra whipped off their hats and said hello.

'I can smell the spices,' Nat said, lifting her head and smelling the air. 'We should see the southern gate shortly.'

They continued arm in arm down the north–south road. Petra stopped occasionally to stare through shop windows. Nat waited patiently for her best friend to lose interest, and then they continued south.

'There it is,' Petra said, pointing her chin at the gate. 'And are those the market stalls underneath it?'

Nat skipped forward. 'Yes, that's the market. Come on. We haven't got all day.'

With a chuckle, Petra increased her stride. The shouts of stall-holders selling their goods pierced the morning air.

'Look at this,' Petra said, walking up to a stall filled with beads. 'They are so beautiful.'

The stallholder eyed Petra suspiciously. 'Has your master given you a list?'

Petra frowned. 'I beg your pardon?'

'This is Ernest's daughter,' Nat said, interrupting. 'We are here exploring the market.'

'I am sorry, my lady,' the stallholder spluttered. 'Please, take what you wish as an apology.'

Petra picked up a small-beaded bracelet and placed it on her wrist. She reached down into her purse and retrieved a copper. She raised an eyebrow at the storekeeper and placed the coin on the table.

The stallholder stared at the coin as if it would suddenly come alive and attack him. 'I am sorry, my lady.'

Petra smiled. 'No harm done, sir. Thank you for my bracelet.'

'Let's go,' Nat said, pulling Petra away. 'I think his head is going to explode.'

Petra slowed Nat down and surveyed the market area. A deep frown was etched on her forehead.

'What is it, my lady?' Nat said.

'Every stall has a man behind it,' Petra said. 'And everyone buying goods seems to be a woman with a list.'

'There's so much you don't know, Petra,' Nat said. 'This is the way in Fairacre. Women are property. You will find out soon enough. Just wait till you get married.'

Petra snorted. 'I shall never be property.'

Nat smirked at her friend. 'No. I doubt you will ever be property. The poor, poor man.'

'My lady,' Greta said, appearing from behind a market stall and bowing deeply. 'Are these men behaving themselves?'

'Shut it, Greta,' a stallholder growled.

Greta showed the man a rude sign.

'She definitely isn't property,' Petra said. 'How are you, Greta? I am pleased to meet you.'

'Oh, you know, living the dream, free as a bird,' Greta said, doing a jig.

'Homeless and hungry,' a stallholder shouted.

Greta snorted. 'Don't listen to that old fool. How are you enjoying the market?'

'It is wonderful,' Petra said. 'I am going to spend some more time exploring and after, I wish to go to the weaving district.'

Greta pulled her lips into a tight line. 'Are you sure you want to, my lady?'

Petra lifted her eyes to the sky. 'Why does everyone keep treating me like a child?'

'We just want you to be safe,' Nat said, resting a hand on Petra's forearm.

'I will guide you,' Greta said. 'For a fee, of course.'

'That would be wonderful,' Petra said, clapping her hands. 'I am going to explore the rest of the stalls and then we can begin.'

An hour later, Petra walked north of the market stalls up to where Nat and Greta stood. 'Are we ready?'

'We are ready, my lady,' Nat said.

'It is very important you do not go into any of the alleys,' Greta said. 'It is not safe for you there.'

Petra looked at Nat, who gave her a nod. 'OK, I will do as you say,' Petra said to Greta. 'I don't want to cause any trouble.'

Greta extended her hand, palm up.

'Payment,' Nat said.

'Oh,' Petra said, reaching into her purse and pulling out a silver. Before she could hand it over, Nat grabbed her hand.

'A copper now, and a copper once we are done,' Nat said.

'Spoilsport,' Greta said, taking the copper from Petra. 'Please follow me, my lady.'

They walked up the north–south road until they reached a road that turned right. Then they entered the weaving district. On either side, the tall walls of houses and shops blocked out the sun. They followed the winding street until they reached a crossroads. Greta turned to the south.

'Is that an alley?' Petra said, pointing to a dark area between two tall houses.

'Yes, my lady,' Greta said, peering over her shoulder. 'The

alleys were my home before I found work in the entertainment district.'

'Your home?' Petra said, with a confused look.

Greta glanced at Nat.

'She doesn't come here often, Greta,' Nat said. 'We can talk about this after we have left the weaving district. Let's continue, shall we?'

The street wound south. The walls of the houses and shops came closer together, then parted, as the street widened, then narrowed. Women stood in shop doorways and glared as Petra walked by. Clothes of all types adorned window mannequins.

'Do you wish to explore the shops, my lady?' Greta said.

'I would like to look at wedding dresses,' Petra said.

'They're on the east–west road,' Greta said. 'We will make our way to the southern wall, then go to the eastern gate.'

They reached a crossroads where a single light flickered, and walked past a shop with 'Arts and Crafts' written above the door. A 'We are closed' sign hung on the inside of the door. They turned south and made for the southern wall.

Petra stopped walking.

'What is it?' Nat said, looking around with concern.

'I hear children,' Petra said, looking around.

'In the alleys,' Greta said. 'They offer no threat, my lady.'

'Children in the alleys?' Petra said. 'Why are there children in the alleys?'

After Greta gave Nat a confused look, she turned to Petra and said, 'It is their home, my lady. It is where all the discarded girls live.'

Petra's mouth hung open. 'What on earth do you mean, discarded girls?'

'This is not the place to talk about these things,' Nat said, grabbing Petra by the arm. 'We can talk when we get home.'

'We are also being followed,' Greta said, glancing up the road. 'We need to keep moving.'

The three women increased their strides until they reached the southern wall.

'Who is following us?' Petra whispered as they turned east.

'There is a man in a cloak,' Greta said. 'And a few drunks who prowl the streets. They are quick to rob you of your coin.'

Petra glanced over her shoulder.

'We will be OK if we stick together and stay in the sunlight,' Greta said. 'They won't dare do anything with shop owners watching.'

The southern wall on their right shoulder loomed high into the sky. The buildings this far south stood worn and broken. Some lay empty.

'Look at that place,' Petra said, pointing to a tall four-storey building. 'It is much higher than the rest.'

'It used to be a school,' Greta said. 'They closed it down when they moved the schools to the cliffs.'

'Why is it empty?' Petra said. 'Can they not use it for something else?'

Greta shrugged. 'I don't know, my lady. I bet it's unsafe inside, though. Lots of weird people hiding in there.'

They continued walking east until they reached the wall. They turned north with the eastern wall on their right shoulder. Up in the distance, the eastern gate rose into the sky.

Halfway up the eastern wall, Petra stopped again and peered down an alley.

'What is it?' Nat said, moving close to Petra.

Petra pointed at eyes looking out from the darkness.

Nat shivered. 'Who is it?'

'Just a small girl hiding in the shadows,' Greta said. 'It's not safe to stop here. We should continue.'

Petra looked one more time into the alley, shook her head, then continued north.

'You are quiet, my lady?' Nat said.

Petra scrunched up her nose and gave Nat a half smile. 'I cannot stop thinking about the girls in the alleys.'

'It would be best to forget them,' Greta said. 'It is the way of the South and it will never change.'

'Hmm,' Petra said, her eyes staring into the distance.

They reached the eastern gate. Greta skipped over to the gate guards and began teasing them. Petra peered through the gate at the neat lines of trees in the distance.

'The orchards,' Nat said. 'Your father owns most of them.'

Petra placed her hand on her forehead to block out the sun. 'I would like to visit the orchards one day.'

'My lady,' Peter said, walking up behind them. 'I see you have survived your tour of the weaving district.'

'We have,' Petra said. 'I am unimpressed with what is happening in the alleys though, Captain.'

Nat gave Petra a stern look. 'We shouldn't be bringing this up with the captain of Fairacre, my lady.'

'We will try to clean them up,' the young captain said with a bow. 'What is your next port for exploration?'

'Wedding dresses, then lunch in the entertainment district,' Nat said.

The young captain looked at Nat and turned a slight pink.

'We need to go,' Nat said, grabbing Petra's hand and pulling her away.

'Be careful, ladies,' Peter called after them.

'He is totally in love with you. You need to tell him you cannot be with him,' Petra said. 'You will break his heart otherwise.'

'I am afraid his heart is going to break anyway,' Nat said, sighing. 'As much fun as it is, I didn't want to hurt anyone.'

'Here we are, my lady,' Greta said, running up behind them and pointing to a large shop window.

'Oh my,' Petra said, placing a hand over her mouth. 'Look at those dresses, Nat.'

'Beautiful,' Nat said. 'Come on. Let's try some on.'

The doorbell tinkled as Petra opened the door. She walked into the shop and stopped at the counter. A group of men turned and stared.

'My lady.' The shop owner bowed after giving Greta a look of disdain. 'My name is Arnold. May I be of help?'

'We are here to try on wedding dresses,' Nat said. 'We are both to be married in the spring.'

'Excellent,' Arnold said, clapping his hands. 'Only the two of you, I assume.'

'Yes, Arnold, just those two,' Greta said, looking up at the ceiling. 'I guess I will wait outside.'

Petra and Nat looked at each other with raised eyebrows.

'Refused my hand in marriage, she did,' Arnold muttered, as he beckoned them past the counter. 'Brought great shame on me and my house.'

'You wanted to marry Greta?' Petra said, following Arnold to the centre of the shop.

Arnold nodded over his shoulder. 'I did, my lady. She said no. I was the laughing stock of Fairacre. A man who owns the greatest wedding shop in the whole of our land gets refused marriage. It was very embarrassing.'

'That is very sad,' Petra said.

'I eventually found a new wife,' Arnold said. 'And made sure nobody would ever go near Greta again.'

'She is not allowed to marry?' Petra said.

'She is allowed to marry,' Arnold said. 'But no man will risk her saying no to him. She will never, ever marry.'

'That is also sad,' Nat said.

Arnold eyed Nat. 'She should not have refused.'

Petra opened her mouth to say something, then thought better of it.

'Here we are, my lady,' Arnold said, pointing at a small bench. 'If you could stand on the pedestal and I will take your measurements.'

Petra stood on the pedestal and lifted her arms. Arnold took her measurements, then Nat's. He disappeared into the back of his shop.

'Are you OK?' Nat said, as they both sat waiting for Arnold.

Petra let out a sigh. 'The more I see what happens to women in this town, the more angry I get.'

Nat lifted an eyebrow. 'That isn't like you. You have always said we should know our place.'

'I think maybe I come from a different place than most women,' Petra said.

A snort escaped Nat's nose. 'Oh, you think, do you?'

Petra bit her bottom lip and placed her hand on her belly.

'It's OK,' Nat said as she pushed Petra's hand away from her stomach. 'Let's try on some wedding dresses and then go to lunch.'

'Here you go,' Arnold said, walking under a mountain of white material.

Petra and Nat spent the next few hours trying on wedding dresses. The men in the shop nodded in approval as Petra appeared from the fitting room. Nat shed a tear because Petra bought her a wedding dress as a birthday present. After giving their address for delivery, they thanked Arnold and left his shop.

'Where do you think Greta got to?' Petra said, as they stepped outside.

'She will find us,' Nat said, steering Petra to the west. 'Let's go to the entertainment district and get some food. I am starving.'

On the way down the east–west road, Petra and Nat stopped at a few more shops where they bought clothes. At the town square, they turned south, walked a few blocks, then turned right through the main gates into the entertainment district.

Where the market was full of people shouting the prices of their wares, the entertainment district sang with the choruses of drunk people having a good time.

'There is a place at the end of the main road,' Nat said. 'Harold told me to take you there.'

A few minutes later, they walked up a small bank of grass and entered a diner with outdoor seating. After ordering a meal and drinks, they sat at an outside table and watched the partying below them.

'Did you see that?' Petra said, placing her hand on her brow before narrowing her eyes.

'Children running out of alleys looking for scraps,' Greta said from behind them.

Nat jumped and slammed her knee on the table. She sucked in a quick breath and scrunched up her eyes.

'I am so sorry,' Greta said. 'I didn't mean to startle you.'

Petra bit her bottom lip to stop herself from laughing.

'What's so funny?' Nat said, rubbing her knee furiously.

'Are you OK?' Petra said. 'I didn't know you were such a scaredy-cat.'

'I am fine,' Nat said, pouting at Petra.

Petra placed her hand on her brow again and stared into the entertainment district. 'I cannot see the children.'

'They are quick, my lady,' Greta said. 'Probably scrounging for food.'

A waiter walked up, shoved Greta aside, and placed food and drink on the table. He looked at Greta and snarled.

'Please can you get my friend a plate of food and a drink?' Petra said, nodding at Greta.

The waiter looked at her, then back at Petra. 'I beg your pardon?'

'I said, can you get a plate of food for my friend?' Petra repeated. 'I am sure that is not a problem?'

The waiter turned on his heel and stormed into the diner.

'I think you need to calm down, Petra,' Nat said, glancing over her shoulder. 'Misbehaving like this will get back to your father.'

'Let it get back to him,' Petra said. 'He will certainly hear about this from me when we get home, anyway. Come and sit with us, Greta.'

Greta looked around nervously. 'I shouldn't, my lady. I occasionally work here. Word will get back to my boss and he won't let me work here anymore.'

'Then I will speak to your boss,' Petra said. 'Sit, please.'

Greta pulled out a chair and sat. A minute later, the waiter returned and placed a plate of food in front of her. No sooner had the plate hit the table than Greta grabbed some of the food and shoved it into her mouth.

'Hungry, I see,' Petra said.

With a mouth full of food, Greta said, 'I am starving.'

They sat in silence throughout the meal. Petra kept her eyes trained on the alleys down in the entertainment district. She would occasionally mutter something under her breath and shake her head.

'That was lovely,' Greta said.

Petra pushed her plate over to Greta. 'Have the rest of this.'

Greta grabbed the plate and continued eating.

A shout made Greta look up from her food. Petra threw a

hand up to her mouth. Down below, near an alley, a man stood shaking a young girl by the ear. Loud shouts floated up to the diner.

Petra stood and balled her hands into fists.

'Leave it alone, Petra,' Nat said. 'You will just cause more trouble.'

'I will not ignore it,' Petra said, leaving the table and striding down the grass hill.

'Thieves, the lot of you!' the man shouted. 'I am going to throw you into jail.'

'You let her go,' Petra said, walking up to the man.

The man sneered at Petra. His yellow broken teeth and unshaven face made Petra place her hand over her mouth.

'Or what?' the man said, shaking the girl harder.

Petra closed in on him and raised a hand. 'Let her go.'

The man let the young girl go and turned his attention to Petra. 'You should know your place, woman.'

'Don't you dare speak to me like that,' Petra said.

The man spat on the ground in front of her.

With a growl deep in her throat, Petra took a step forward and threw a hand at the man's face. He caught her arm and twisted.

'You are hurting me,' Petra said, her knees buckling.

A loud crunch of bone sounded through the entertainment district. Petra's arm was suddenly free. The drunkard lay face down in a heap on the ground.

'My lady, are you OK?'

Petra burst into tears and threw her arms around Harold's neck.

'You are safe, my lady,' Harold said, turning and guiding Petra back towards the diner.

'This is who has been following us,' Greta said, jabbing a finger into Harold's chest. 'I have seen that cloak all day long.'

Petra sat next to Nat and wiped the tears from her face.

'Are you OK?' Nat said, placing an arm over Petra's shoulder. 'I told you not to go down there.'

After a few deep breaths, Petra calmed her beating heart. She looked at Harold. 'Is it true? Have you been following us?'

Harold bowed his head but kept quiet.

'I think we should talk about that when we get home,' Nat said.

Petra looked back into the entertainment district. The man who Harold had struck was no longer there. The entrance to the alley lay empty. A moment later, she turned to Greta. 'I saw the state of the young girl in that alley. She looked near death.'

Greta shrugged. 'Most of them are, my lady. It is a hard life living in the alleys.'

'How many young girls live there?' Petra said.

'I think we should go home,' Harold said, with a worried glance down the grass bank.

Petra raised a hand. 'I want to know, Harold. I don't want this hidden from me.'

Greta thought for a moment. 'I think just shy of fifty girls, my lady.'

'Fifty?' Petra said, raising her voice.

'There may be more I don't know,' Greta said. 'Fairacre is big, with a lot of alleys.'

Petra dropped her head into her hands. 'How can this be? How can the town I love treat girls so badly?'

'It has always been this way,' Nat said.

'Is this why you agreed to be my father's servant, Harold?' Petra said. 'Was my mother destined for the alleys?'

'We know you are Petra's grandfather, Harold,' Nat said, placing a hand on his forearm.

The Adam's apple in Harold's throat bobbed. After a few seconds, he cleared his throat. 'Yes, my lady. My daughter, your mother, was to be sent to the alleys.'

'And you sacrificed everything to save her?' Petra said.

Harold looked away.

Petra reached out and pulled Harold into a hug. 'We will speak more of this. But now, can you take me home?'

Harold offered his hands to both Petra and Nat.

Petra took Harold's hand and stood. She looked at Greta. 'Thank you for your help today. Here is the copper coin. I would like to have your help in the future.'

Greta pocketed the copper. 'Just send a runner to find me, my lady.'

Harold led the two women through the entertainment district and onto the north–south road. They made their way around the town square, then began the climb up the steep hill.

'I am going to do something about those girls,' Petra said as they ascended.

Nat looped her arm around Petra's.

'I promise you, Nat,' Petra said. 'No child should have to live like that.'

'Be smart about it, my lady,' Nat said. 'Remember what you are up against.'

'Be very smart,' Harold said. 'The men in this town will not take kindly to this.'

'Then I shall be smart,' Petra said. 'Tomorrow, I will plan.'

They reached the house in the late afternoon. Petra thought about speaking to her father, then heard the heated discussions in the trades room. With a goodnight to Nat and Harold, she retired to her wing of the house.

CHAPTER 3
'I DO NOT CARE FOR LAWS

'Who's there?' Petra said.

Children's giggles sounded outside the window.

Petra slipped out of bed and stumbled over to see what was going on. She peered into the moonlit backyard. A shadow of a small child flashed against the western wall. Petra yanked the window's handle and cursed as the metal dug into her flesh. The fresh evening air made goosebumps run along her arms. More giggles whispered through the air.

Petra leant out of the window. 'Hello? Who is there?'

The patter of tiny feet echoed off the tall western wall. A gust of wind shook the trees. Another giggle floated through the air.

Petra closed the window, marched over to her dresser, and put on the clothes she had worn that day. She left her room and quietly double-stepped down the staircase. The moonlight beamed into the living room through large windows. Petra made her way to the double back doors and peered into the garden. Seeing nobody, she walked out and crossed the garden until she reached the western wall. A giggle sounded to her left.

'Come out here,' Petra said as she stood on her toes to look over the fence. 'I will not hurt you.'

Four eyes appeared out of the darkness. Then, in a flash, they disappeared. Petra followed the western wall until she reached the thick wooden fence. She stood on her tiptoes again and peered over the fence. A thin pathway followed the western wall. Petra walked back up the garden along the fence until she reached the small gate. After exiting through the gate, she followed the fence back to the western wall. At the wall, she turned down the narrow dark path, keeping the wall on her right shoulder.

The pitter patter of bare feet sounded from the dark path.

'Where are you?' Petra said, walking slowly. 'Are you OK?'

'Shh,' a young girl said. 'She is following us.'

'I will not hurt you,' Petra said. 'Can we talk? Where are you?'

More giggles sounded from further down the narrow path.

Petra took a deep breath, wrapped her arms around herself, and quick-stepped down the path. The pitter patter of bare feet on cobbles bounced off the western wall. The path continued steeply as Petra moved down through the northern district.

'Please stop running,' Petra said. 'All I want to do is to talk to you.'

'Quick, run,' a girl said.

Petra caught two tiny figures disappearing down an alley.

'Hide,' a girl's voice said.

Petra narrowed her eyes to get a better look. A few moments later, she walked into the alley then crouched. Slowly, her eyes adjusted.

Out of the darkness, eyes of all different shapes and sizes stared back at her.

Petra took in a sharp breath and fell onto her backside.

Two girls stepped from the shadows. Ripped oversized boys'

clothes hung off their shoulders. Toes poked out of holes in the boys' shoes they were wearing.

'You led her into the alley, silly,' a girl said, swiping her hand at the other.

The young girl folded her arms and pouted.

'What's your name?' Petra said to the eldest as she got to her feet.

'Why should I tell you?' the older girl said, raising her chin. 'You are a rich one from the north. A rich person who doesn't care about us.'

Petra moved a few paces forward, then sat on a piece of cardboard. 'I do care about you. I didn't know you all lived here. What is your name?'

'We live on your doorstep,' the girl said. 'How can you not know we live here?'

'I am sorry,' Petra said, spreading her hands. 'I am here now. What is your name?'

'Fay,' the older girl said.

'I am Harriet,' the young girl said.

'Shh,' Fay said, clipping Harriet around the ear. 'The lady hasn't asked you your name yet.'

'Sorry,' Harriet said, looking down at the ground.

'And what is your name?' Petra said, looking at Harriet.

Harriet's face brightened. 'My name is Harriet. With two Rs.'

'OK, Harriet-with-two-Rs,' Petra said. 'It is nice to meet you.'

'Nice to meet you too, rich lady,' Harriet said.

Fay lifted her chin and continued to look at Petra with suspicion.

'So, Fay and Harriet,' Petra said. 'How long have you lived here in the alleys?'

Harriet shrugged.

'They left Harriet here when she was a baby,' Fay said.

'And what about you, Fay?' Petra said.

Fay dropped her head and looked at her hands. 'I can't remember.'

Petra peered at all the girls lying around in the alley. Some lay under boxes. Some sat against the walls. All of them were staring wide-eyed at Petra.

'What you looking at?' Harriet said, placing her hands on her hips.

Petra gave Harriet a sad smile. 'I am wondering how many of you are here in the alleys?'

Harriet opened her arms wide. 'There are lots and lots and lots.'

'I can see that,' Petra said. 'All ages and sizes.'

'Fay is one of the oldest,' a girl said. 'There is a black girl somewhere who is as old as Fay.'

'What is her name?' Petra said.

Harriet shrugged. 'Don't know.'

'We don't say anything we shouldn't say, miss,' someone said. 'We will get into trouble.'

'How will you get into trouble?' Petra said.

'The snatchers come,' the girl said. 'They come and take us away to clean the streets. We don't last long cleaning the streets, miss.'

'Why are you here, miss?' Fay said.

'I followed you here,' Petra said. 'It looks like Harriet was playing in my garden.'

Fay clipped Harriet on the back of the head again. 'You shouldn't be out there.'

Harriet scowled up at Fay. 'I was just playing.'

'I have a question for you both,' Petra said. 'You don't have to answer if you don't want to.'

Fay and Harriet remained silent. Their suspicious eyes did not blink.

'If I were to have a big house where we could all live, would you come and stay with me?'

Fay raised an eyebrow and folded her arms.

'Oh, can we, Fay?' Harriet said, looking up at her.

'We couldn't, miss,' a girl said. 'The snatchers would come for us.'

'Are you working for the snatchers?' Fay said.

'No, I am not working for the snatchers,' Petra said. 'Why don't these snatchers come and take you all now?'

'They can only take us if we do something bad,' a girl said. 'Like steal some food.'

Petra pulled her legs underneath her. She rested her elbows on her knees and her chin on her fist. She looked slowly at each of the girls lying or sitting in front of her.

'Why are you staring?' Harriet said.

'I think you can come to the house because you haven't done anything wrong,' Petra said.

'Fay,' Harriet said. 'We can go with the miss.'

Fay shook her head. 'I don't think it is a good idea. I think we will all have done a bad thing and the snatchers will take us.'

'I would never do that to you,' Petra said. 'I will get the house, anyway. Once I get it, you can sneak in and come and look if you want.'

'Yes, yes, can we, Fay?' Harriet said, tugging on Fay's clothes. 'We can have a room. I have never had a room.'

The breath caught in Petra's throat. 'Of course. You would never have had your own room, would you?'

Harriet smiled. 'It is OK. I have a box. I clean it every day, don't I, Fay?'

'Yes, you do, little one,' Fay said, rubbing Harriet's hair. 'And a good job you do, too.'

'Who goes there?' a man's voice shouted.

'Snatcher,' Harriet whispered, then disappeared into the darkness. The girls scattered. A second later, the alley was quiet.

'I said, who goes there?'

Petra walked out of the alley.

'What are you doing here, lady?' a guard said. 'You shouldn't be out here.'

'Maybe she is helping these filthy, rotten girls,' another guard said as he walked behind her.

The guard in front of her pulled out a short baton. 'Is that what you are doing? Feeding these thieving children?'

The slap of the baton in hand made Petra flinch. 'My name is Petra. I am Ernest's daughter.'

'Sure you are, pretty lady,' the guard said. 'And I am the king of the City of Lynn.'

The guard behind snorted, then chuckled.

'I am warning you,' Petra said. 'If you lay a finger on me, my father will have your heads.'

'Your father isn't bigger than the laws of Fairacre,' the guard said. 'You are in an alley after dark. We are going to tie you up and take you to the town jail.'

'You will do no such thing,' Petra said.

The guard behind Petra lunged and grabbed her by the arm.

'Let go of me,' Petra shouted. 'You are hurting me.'

'Nobody can hear you, pretty lady,' the guard said. 'And even if they did, they wouldn't come to help you.'

'Let her go,' a girl shouted, jumping out of the alley.

A sickening crunch sounded. The girl crumpled to the ground.

'What have you done?' Petra screamed. 'You have killed her.'

'She is sleeping and will wake up with a sore head,' the guard said. 'I think I will take her to jail with you.'

With a growl, Petra pulled her head back and swung her forehead at the guard's nose. Another sickening crunch sounded through the alley.

The guard stumbled back. 'You broke my nose,' he said, with a hand full of blood.

Petra held her hand on her forehead as she swayed on her feet.

'You will pay for that,' the guard said, taking a step forward and swinging his baton.

Petra fell backwards. Her scream caught in her throat as the baton slammed into her thigh. Her leg buckled, but the second guard caught her and held her up.

'You won't dodge this one,' the guard said, lifting his baton and aiming it at Petra's head.

A flutter sounded through the alley. The guard standing in front of Petra suddenly fell into a heap. The guard behind Petra kicked her forward and drew his sword. Petra fell to the ground and rolled onto her back. A large man in a cloak stepped over her.

'Who are you?' the guard hissed.

The man pulled out a long, thin sword. A second later, the sound of steel meeting steel rang through the alley. The guard's sword found its mark and sliced across the man's forearm. With a feint to the side, the man flicked his sword and hit the guard in the throat. Blood trickled down his neck.

'OK, OK, please don't hurt me,' the guard said, sheathing his sword.

'Take your friend and get out of here,' Harold said.

The guard lifted his partner over his shoulder and walked down the narrow road.

Harold turned and offered Petra a hand. Petra took it and

pulled herself up. She gripped his shoulder to stop the world from swaying.

'You shouldn't be out here, my lady.'

'Harold?' Petra said. 'Is that you?'

Harold unclipped his mask. 'Yes, my lady. We need to get you home.'

'You saved me, Grandpapa,' Petra said, her head falling onto Harold's chest.

Harold wrapped his arm around Petra and walked her to the western wall.

'You are bleeding,' Petra said.

'We can look at it when we get home,' Harold said. 'No doubt the guards have gone to find friends. We need to get out of here as quickly as possible.'

Petra looked over her shoulder. 'What about the girl?'

'She is awake,' Harold said. 'The other girls will look after her. They are used to dealing with that type of thing.'

Petra's chest heaved as the tears started to flow. 'Have you seen how they live, Grandpapa? Have you?'

A rumble sounded deep in Harold's chest. 'I have seen how they live. What this town has done to those young girls—'

'You did good by my mama,' Petra said. 'You saved her from that. From living like that, didn't you?'

Harold cleared his throat. 'I think you will find your father saved her from that. I was just someone to sweeten the deal.'

'Mama didn't want to be with Papa,' Petra said. 'She must have hated going to live with him.'

'It was a lot better than being discarded in the alleys,' Harold said.

They continued along the western wall until they reached the high fence. They followed the fence to the gate, which Harold held open while Petra stepped through. The grass crunched as they walked to the back door. Petra let out a gasp as two eyes stared at her through the big window next to the door.

'Where have you two been?' Nat said, opening the back door.

'You scared me. Can we get Harold indoors?' Petra said. 'He has an injury, Nat.'

'It is nothing,' Harold said.

Nat grabbed his hand and pulled him to the kitchen. 'Sit,' she said, pointing to a stool.

Harold sat and stared straight ahead as Nat worked on his wounds.

'Is he going to be OK?' Petra said.

'It's deep, but we have caught it early,' Nat said. 'What were you doing out there?'

Petra ran Nat through the events of the evening. 'Those poor girls, Nat. They live tired, hungry, cold and in fear.'

'Right now, I am more interested in the two soldiers that came after you,' Nat said, her voice rising. 'I will have a word with Peter about that.'

Harold's brow creased. 'I don't think that is a good idea, Nat. Petra and I will have a lot of explaining to do.'

Nat looked at Petra, then back at Harold. She cursed under her breath.

Petra pulled up a chair and sat next to Harold. 'What are these clothes you are wearing?'

Harold unclipped the cloak and handed it to Petra. 'Your mother was an expert weaver. She made these clothes for me a long time ago.'

Petra pulled the cloak over her shoulders and raised the hood over her head.

'Now, click the mask into place,' Harold said, pointing to the clip inside the hood.

Petra reached inside and pulled the mask over her face. She clicked the strap into place.

'It suits you,' Nat said with a smile. 'With the right clothes, it will be very hard to spot you.'

'I just need the black hugging clothes to go with it, then I will look the part,' Petra said.

'I can arrange it,' Harold said.

'Where did you come from when those soldiers had me? It is like you appeared out of nowhere.'

'From the roof, my lady,' Harold said. 'It is easy to traverse Fairacre on the flat rooftops.'

'I demand you take me and Nat with you one day,' Petra said. 'I want to see how you get around Fairacre.'

Harold raised an eyebrow. 'If you get caught, you will land yourself in a lot of trouble.'

'We just won't get caught then, will we?' Nat said. 'There, I have wrapped the wound. We need to change that bandage every day for the next week.'

'How does it feel?' Petra said.

'I will survive,' Harold said.

Petra stood and wrapped her arms around Harold's neck. 'Thanks again for saving me, Grandpapa.'

A small smile played across Harold's lips.

'I think it is time for both of you to get some rest,' Nat said.

Harold narrowed his eyes. 'Remember, we cannot tell anybody about this. I am afraid it will bring a large amount of pain to all of us.'

'I so want to speak to Peter about those soldiers,' Nat said. 'But I won't.'

'I won't say anything,' Petra said. 'But I will not sit around and let those children live like that.'

Both Harold and Nat sighed.

'What?' Petra said.

'You won't let this go, will you?' Nat said. 'I think there are difficult times ahead.'

'You are right,' Petra said, standing up and walking to the kitchen door. 'It is going to be difficult and I will not let this go.'

Harold and Nat sighed again.

'Goodnight,' Petra said.

'What happened to you?' Ernest said, raising an eyebrow at Harold.

'I lost a fight with a kitchen knife, sir,' Harold said as he poured Ernest another coffee.

'You cut your forearm with a kitchen knife?' Ernest said, frowning.

Harold glanced at his forearm. 'It was a freak accident, sir.'

Ernest shook his head.

'What are you doing today, Papa?' Petra said, smiling at her father to distract him.

Ernest turned to Petra. 'I am going to the orchards for the day. Is there something you need?'

'No, I am good, thanks,' Petra said. 'We are going to continue exploring Fairacre.'

'Please be careful,' Ernest said, rising from the breakfast table. 'I hear someone assaulted some guards last night. Fairacre is full of dark places, which can be dangerous. Especially for a woman.'

Petra pursed her lips. 'I will be extra careful, Father.'

Ernest gave his daughter a nod and disappeared out of the kitchen. A moment later, the front door opened and closed as he left for the orchard.

'That was a close one,' Nat said, looking at Harold.

'He knows something is going on,' Harold said. 'Your father always knows what's going on.'

Petra pushed her chair back. 'I know, but he doesn't know what I will do next.'

'Oh?' Nat said. 'What are you up to?'

'I am off to the town hall,' Petra said, walking out. 'I will be leaving in the next five minutes.'

Harold and Nat glanced at each other, then quickly made their way to their quarters to get changed. Five minutes later, the three stepped out into the morning sunshine.

'What are you up to, Petra?' Nat said, hooking her arm into Petra's.

'I am going to sort out a home for the young children in the alleys.'

Harold increased his stride until he was alongside Petra. 'How are you planning to do that?'

Petra glanced at her grandfather. 'I will purchase the old school in the south of Fairacre.'

'You cannot purchase property, my lady,' Harold said. 'The law forbids it.'

'We will see about that,' Petra said, increasing her stride. 'I am getting very tired of being told what I can and cannot do.'

The road flattened as they came to the end of the northern district. The town hall and library loomed up ahead. Petra continued into the square, then climbed the stairs to the town hall's front doors.

'Halt,' a guard said, moving his spear across the door.

'I wish to enter and speak to Hargreaves,' Petra said. 'Let me in.'

The guard stood unmoving.

Harold stepped forward. 'I wish to speak to Hargreaves. I represent Ernest and his trading businesses.'

The guard immediately stepped back and removed his spear.

'I request that my two friends accompany me,' Harold said.

The guard gave him a single nod.

'You do know I am Ernest's daughter,' Petra said to the guard.

The guard ignored her.

'My lady, please,' Harold said, showing the way through the door. 'The guard is under orders.'

With a growl, Petra stepped forward. As they walked through the town hall, men stopped talking to stare. Petra increased her stride, lifted her chin, and gazed forward. They reached the back of the town hall and walked through the double doors into the long corridor. At the end of the corridor, Harold rapped his knuckles on the mayor's door.

'Come,' Hargreaves said.

Harold opened the doors and waved the girls through.

Hargreaves's chair bashed against the wall as he stood. 'What are you lot doing here?'

From a big leather chair in front of the mayor's desk, Peter spun and frowned. 'And how did you get into the town hall?'

'That will be my fault,' Harold said, raising his hand. 'Petra was determined to see you, Hargreaves.'

Hargreaves walked over to Petra and grabbed her hand. 'How can we help you, my lady?'

'I want to buy the old school in the south of Fairacre,' Petra said.

'You what?' Hargreaves said, both eyebrows raising.

Petra pulled out her purse and dropped it onto the desk. 'I want to buy the old school. I have the money to purchase it.'

Hargreaves looked at Peter.

'You are not allowed to,' Peter said, while pushing himself out of the chair. 'Do you not understand?'

'I do not care if Fairacre's laws forbid me,' Petra said, folding her arms. 'I have the money. Please do the paperwork so I can purchase the property.'

'The law does not allow it,' Peter said, his voice lowering. 'And right now I have reports of two of my guards lying in hospital beds. Do you know anything about that?'

Petra glanced at Harold.

'Do you know anything about it, sir?' Peter said, looking at Harold's arm.

Harold looked into the distance and stood still.

'Answer me, please, sir,' Peter said.

'What is wrong with you, Peter?' Nat said. 'Why would Harold have anything to do with your guards?'

Peter stood his ground. 'Where were you last night, sir?'

'He was at home with me,' Petra said.

Peter faced Petra. 'There was a report of a rich woman walking through the alleys. Where were you last night?'

Petra folded her arms. 'I don't have to answer to you.'

'I can take you to the jail, where you will have to answer to me,' Peter said.

'Peter, what is wrong with you?' Nat said. 'It's Petra and Harold. Have you lost your mind?'

The couch hissed as Peter dropped into it. He folded his arms, closed his eyes, and took a deep breath.

'I want to buy the old school, Hargreaves,' Petra said. 'I want you to draw up the paperwork now.'

'You are not allowed to, Petra,' Hargreaves said. 'These are the rules set by the City of Lynn.'

'I don't care what the City of Lynn says,' Petra said, raising her voice.

'Good day,' a man said from the doorway.

'Good morning, Leonard,' Hargreaves said, waving him in. 'How are you?'

Leonard, seeing Nat, turned a bright pink. Peter snorted, then pushed himself deeper into the chair. Nat bit her lip and moved closer to Petra.

'Awkward,' Petra said.

'Petra wants to buy property,' Hargreaves said, quickly interrupting.

Leonard pulled a handkerchief out of his pocket and wiped his forehead. 'Not allowed.'

'This is ridiculous,' Petra said. 'I have the coin. My father is Ernest. He practically owns half of Fairacre. And I cannot buy my own property?'

'You are not a man,' Leonard said. 'City of Lynn's orders.'

'It is wrong though, Leonard,' Nat said.

Leonard's eyes widened. 'Yes, my lady.'

Petra rolled her eyes.

'I will buy it,' Harold said.

Petra turned and stared at Harold. 'You will?'

'I will, but I will need a loan,' Harold said, looking at Petra's purse.

The coins clinked as the purse dropped into Harold's hand.

Harold turned to Leonard and gave him the coin purse. 'I think you will find there is enough coin there, Leonard.'

Leonard bounced the purse in his hand. He opened the drawstring and pulled out four gold coins, which he handed back to Harold. The coin purse bounced one more time in his hand. 'There is the correct amount of coin in the purse now. I will draw up the paperwork. Can I have your details?'

Harold gave Leonard what he needed. Leonard scrunched up his eyes as he frowned.

'Is there something wrong?' Petra said.

Leonard thought for a moment, then shook his head. 'No, everything is OK. I will draw up the paperwork.'

'I will come with you,' Nat said.

Leonard's eyes turned into saucers. 'OK, yes, OK, my lady.'

'Oh, whatever,' Peter said from the couch. 'I will go with you, Leonard.'

Nat and Leonard left the mayor's office, ignoring him.

'Very mature, Peter,' Petra said, shaking her head at him.

'What will you use the building for?' Hargreaves said.

'We are going to convert it into an inn,' Harold said, glancing at Petra. 'An inn for travellers and traders.'

A smile stretched across Petra's face. 'Yes, an inn for traders and travellers, courtesy of my family.'

'It needs a lot of work,' Hargreaves said. 'It is falling apart.'

'I am sure we can hire some people to help us,' Petra said.

Peter pushed himself out of the chair. 'I must see to my guards,' he muttered, walking to the door. 'If you need anything, I will be in the town square.'

'I knew that wouldn't end well,' Hargreaves said after Peter closed the door. 'He is heartbroken.'

Petra bit her bottom lip as she glanced at him. A few moments later, Leonard and Nat entered the room. Nat raised an eyebrow at the empty chair.

'Everything is in order,' Leonard said. 'All you need to do is sign here.'

Harold took the quill from Leonard and signed the document.

'A copy for you,' Leonard said, handing a piece of paper to Harold.

Harold took the paper and placed it in his pocket. 'Thank you, Leonard.'

'My lady, may I request a night off tonight?' Nat said as she hooked her arm in Leonard's.

'Of course you can have the night off,' Petra said. 'But you are still coming to the inn, right?'

Nat smiled. 'I sure am. Let's get going.'

CHAPTER 4
IT'S BARBARIC

'First, we detour to the entertainment district,' Petra said as they exited the town hall. 'We need to get food and pick up Greta.'

Small groups of people milled around the square. When it was their turn to enter the town hall, the guards signalled for them to get in line. Shouts and complaints filled the air as people got tired of waiting.

'Petra, can you slow down?' Nat said, skipping through the square. 'Harold is injured, remember?'

Petra turned and raised a concerned eyebrow. 'Are you OK, Harold?'

Harold smiled thinly. 'I am fine, my lady. If we could just slow down a bit.'

'He isn't fine,' Nat said. 'Look how white he has gone. I think you should go home,' she said to him.

'Nat is right. Why don't you go home and rest?' Petra said, walking up to Harold and turning him around. 'We will be fine, I promise.'

'I don't want you going into the weaving district alone, my lady,' Harold said. 'Not after what has happened.'

'We are going to get Greta,' Petra said. 'There will be three of us.'

'We will be fine, Harold,' Nat said, shooing him away. 'Go on. Go home and rest.'

Harold sighed at Petra, then turned to Nat. 'Don't you dare let her out of your sight. Remember what she means to me.'

'Go on, you grumpy old man,' Nat said, shoving him away. 'I promise you I will make sure she is OK.'

With a small bow at Petra, Harold turned and walked away. Nat walked over to Petra and linked arms.

'You sure he is going to be OK?' Petra said, looking nervously over her shoulder.

'He has survived a lot worse,' Nat said. 'Come on. I am absolutely starving and we need to find Greta.'

They walked down the north–south road and through the gates into the entertainment district. The main road heaved, full of people trying to make their way into bars. After weaving through the crowd, Petra and Nat reached the grassy hill, which they climbed to the diner.

'There she is,' Petra said, pointing at a group of people sitting at a table. 'She seems to be fighting with that man.'

'Oh dear,' Nat said, increasing her pace. 'He looks really angry. I think we need to save her.'

Petra and Nat walked up to the shouting Greta.

'I am warning you, Greta,' a man said. 'You are not allowed to shout at me.'

'Pay up,' Greta shouted. 'I have served your drinks, now pay up.'

The grumbling man reached into his pocket and pulled out two copper coins. 'I am paying you, but don't shout at me.'

'I wouldn't have, if you'd paid me,' Greta shouted even louder.

Petra cleared her throat. 'Everything OK here, Greta?'

'Hello,' Greta said, smiling at her. 'Everything is OK. Would you like some food?'

'Yes please,' Petra said, walking to a separate table.

Greta dropped the menus in front of the two women, then disappeared into the diner. She returned and took their orders of warm bread, chicken broth, and fruit juice. As Petra and Nat ate, they watched the different entertainers walk up and down the road. The crowds cheered their appreciation at the fire breathers, jugglers and magicians.

'Will that be all?' Greta said. 'I can bring back the menus if you want more.'

'That will be all. Thanks, Greta,' Petra said, placing a silver coin on the table. 'The food was lovely.'

'We have some good news, Greta,' Nat said. 'We have the deed to the old school and we are going to turn it into an inn.'

'That is wonderful news,' Greta said, looking around. She moved in closer. 'Does that mean the girls?'

'Yes,' Petra whispered. 'We are going there now and we need you to come with us.'

Greta picked up the silver coin and untied her apron. 'I will be back.'

A moment later, Petra raised an eyebrow at the shouting in the diner.

'I don't think the owner is best pleased with Greta leaving,' Nat said, turning to look over her shoulder. 'It sounds like Greta is going to hurt him.'

Greta stormed out of the diner and up to the table. 'Let's go,' she said. 'Before I make Terence feel very uncomfortable.'

'I am warning you, Greta,' Terence shouted. 'You cannot keep leaving like this.'

Greta turned and made a series of rude signals towards the bar.

Petra shook her head. 'Will you lose your job?'

'Nah, the owner loves me,' Greta said, before turning around and shouting, 'You love me Terence, don't you?'

'Oh my,' Nat said, placing her hand over her mouth as a stream of curse words came through the diner door.

'You see,' Greta said, spreading her hands and smiling. 'He loves me.'

'It's time to go,' Petra said. 'Before we create a scene.'

'Before we create a scene?' Nat said, chuckling. 'I think we are past that. Let's go.'

They walked down the grassy hill, through the entertainment district, and onto the north–south road. They turned towards the marketplace.

'Where is your hunky bodyguard?' Greta said. 'He does know we are going into the weaving district?'

'At home, taking care of Father's business,' Petra said before Nat could say anything. 'We should be OK, shouldn't we?'

'It is mid-afternoon,' Greta said. 'We will only have a couple of hours in the old school before we must leave.'

'We just want to see what it looks like inside,' Petra said. 'I need to know how much of a clean-up it is going to take.'

'A lot,' Greta said, turning into the weaving district. 'And, just to let you know, we are being followed.'

Petra turned and noticed two idle guards looking at them.

'Why are they following us?' Greta said.

'Perhaps Peter has asked them to keep an eye on us?' Nat said.

Greta mumbled something under her breath.

'What, Greta?' Petra said.

'Nothing,' Greta said. 'Let's keep moving.'

They walked single file as the streets narrowed, then widened. At the crossroads by the closed arts and crafts shop, they turned south towards the southern wall. Then they turned left with their right shoulders to the wall.

'There it is,' Petra said, a smile spreading across her face. 'Look how big it is. We can surely get all the girls in there.'

'Be careful when we get in,' Greta said. 'The wood will have rotted and it will be dangerous. Especially the stairs.'

Petra walked up the four steps and pushed against the double doors. With a groan, the doors swung open. Cobwebs covered all four corners of the opening. A trickle of dust fell from the door frame. Nat waved her hand in front of her face, then coughed loudly.

'It's bigger than I thought,' Petra said, walking through the doors. 'Look at the size of the entrance hall.'

'This place will need a lot of work,' Nat said, walking in behind Petra. 'Look at the splintered floor and the stairs. I think this will take months to fix.'

Petra walked up to the staircase that hugged the wall to the first floor. She kicked the side of it and watched dust spring into the air.

'I don't think it's safe going up there,' Nat said.

'Only one way to find out,' Petra said, climbing onto the first step, then the second.

'Seriously, Petra,' Nat said, shaking her head. 'If you have to climb up there, stay away from the splintered steps.'

'It looks run-down, but once we get rid of the dirt and replace some of these planks, I think what lies underneath will surprise us,' Petra said, climbing onto another step.

'How do you propose we fix this place up?' Nat said. 'I am not sure we'll find anyone who'd willingly work in this house.'

'Harold can work that out for us,' Petra said. 'If not Harold, I will speak to my father.'

The three women froze as the echoes of something clattering to the ground reverberated through the house.

'What was that?' Nat whispered.

Petra put a finger on her lips.

They could hear the pitter patter of small feet from the back of the building.

'Fay, Harriet, come out here,' Greta shouted.

The old school stood in silence.

'I said, come out here!' Greta shouted. 'Or you won't get to live here.'

Two heads, one on top of the other, appeared around the door frame. 'What do you mean live here?' Fay said.

'Do we get our own rooms?' Harriet said, her eyes widening.

'Get out here, the pair of you,' Greta said, clapping her hands.

The two girls in their shredded, stinking clothes walked through the door and stood in front of Greta.

'What are you two doing sneaking around?' Greta said, wagging her finger at them.

'We saw you come in,' Fay said. 'It's dangerous. We always stay away from here. We wanted to warn you because we are nice.'

Petra knelt. 'How would you like to help clean this place up?'

Fay crinkled up her nose. 'This place is disgusting.'

'I will help,' Harriet said.

Petra pulled Harriet into a hug. 'If you help, we might be able to get you a bed.'

'My own room?' Harriet said. 'I can bring my box?'

'You won't need your box,' Petra said. 'You will have your own bed.'

Harriet jumped from foot to foot.

'What about the other girls?' Fay said, folding her arms. 'It will be unfair if they don't get a place to stay.'

'There is enough space for everyone,' Petra said. 'But you have to promise you won't tell anyone about this place.'

Men's voices sounded outside. Harriet's eyes went wide. Greta growled under her breath.

'Snatchers,' Fay whispered. 'We must go before they catch us.'

Greta grabbed Petra and Nat, and pulled them towards a room at the back of the building. She quietly closed the door and gestured that they should all kneel behind the kitchen counters with Fay and Harriet. The front door banged open.

'They are in here,' a man said. 'I heard them talking.'

'They are going to snatch us,' Harriet said, wringing her hands.

'I will speak to them,' Petra whispered.

Greta grabbed Petra by the arm and shook her head. 'I wouldn't do that. These men are dangerous. They don't care who you are.'

'They wouldn't dare touch me,' Petra said.

Nat grabbed Petra's other arm. 'If you go out there and they find out what we are doing, there will be no way you can let the children stay here.'

Petra bit her bottom lip, then nodded.

'Fan out and search every room,' a man said. 'Donte will not be pleased if we come home empty-handed.'

Petra's mouth hung open.

'Donte?' Nat hissed. 'What has he got to do with this?'

'I don't know,' Petra said, frowning.

'We need to go,' Fay said. 'They will find us soon.'

'How do we get out of here?' Petra said.

Fay tugged on Petra's sleeve. 'Follow me, I will show you a way.'

Petra, Nat and Greta crouch-walked through the rows of kitchen workbenches until they reached the back wall. A grate on the wall stood half-open.

'We go in there,' Fay said. 'It is the sewers.'

'The sewers?' Petra said. 'I don't think I can go down there. It's full of rats and disgusting things.'

Harriet rolled her eyes.

Fay grabbed the grate and tugged until it came away from the wall. Harriet jumped through the hole and made a loud splash as she hit the bottom.

'Come on,' Fay said, pointing at the hole. 'The snatchers will be here any minute.'

Petra blew out a long breath.

'I will go first,' Nat said, sliding into the hole. 'I will see what it's like.'

The splash of water signalled Nat landing inside the sewer.

'Your turn,' Fay said.

'I can hear them in here,' a man shouted.

Fay's eyes widened. 'Miss, please go into the hole.'

Greta suddenly stood and walked around the kitchen counters. 'Hello, gentlemen. Can I help you?'

'Where are the children?' a man said.

'What children?' Greta said, walking away from where Petra crouched.

'We heard children!' the man shouted.

'Get in the hole,' Fay hissed through her teeth.

Petra climbed into the hole and pushed. She sucked in a sharp breath as she hit the bottom with a splash.

'They are in the sewers,' the man shouted.

Fay splashed down next to Petra.

'Run,' Harriet shouted.

Petra gagged at the rotting smell hitting the back of her throat. She dragged her feet through the water as she tried to keep up with Harriet and Fay. A splash sounded behind them.

'The snatchers are coming,' Fay said, reaching back and tugging Petra's hand. 'We must go faster.'

They went around a bend and the tunnel widened. A ledge on either side of the water appeared. Petra climbed onto the ledge, then ran after Fay, Harriet and Nat. The tunnels twisted and turned. The men's footsteps grew louder as they gained on them.

Suddenly, Fay disappeared into a dark hole. 'Down here,' she said. 'We hide in the dark.'

The four crouched in a small tunnel. Harriet and Fay placed a hand over their mouths. A few moments later, the footsteps of a man splashed past.

'Let's go,' Fay said, after the footsteps quietened.

They climbed out of the small tunnel and continued down the larger tunnel until they reached a crossroads. Fay held up a hand and listened. A moment later, she pointed to the right tunnel. They all followed it until they reached a dead end where a steel ladder climbed the wall.

'Up here,' Fay said. 'It will lead to an alley.'

Nat climbed up the ladder and stopped. 'There is another grate up here.'

'Push it,' Fay said. 'It will come off.'

With both hands, Nat pushed until the grate clattered to the ground. One by one, they climbed out into the dark alley.

'That was close,' Fay said as she replaced the grate.

Harriet rubbed her arms. 'The snatchers are horrible.'

'I hope Greta is OK,' Nat said.

'I am sure she will be fine,' Petra said. 'She can talk her way out of anything. Don't ever make me go into that sewer again, you hear?'

'You there,' a man shouted.

'What now?' Nat said, turning in the direction of the men's voices.

'We will find you, rich lady,' Harriet said, as she slunk into the shadows. 'We will find you and help you clean the new inn.'

'OK,' Petra whispered. 'Be safe.'

'Come out of there right now,' a guard shouted.

Petra and Nat walked out of the alley.

'That's them,' a man said.

Petra turned and gasped. 'What have you done to Greta?'

'Nothing that won't heal,' a man said, throwing Greta to the ground. 'Where are the children?'

Petra took two steps towards the man and narrowed her eyes. 'I am not telling you a thing. And how dare you hurt Greta!'

The man slapped Petra in the face. 'How dare you speak to me like that! I will have you thrown in jail.'

Petra held her hand to her cheek.

Nat turned to the guards. 'Why are you not doing anything?'

Petra eyed the two guards. They stood with their arms folded. She recognised them from the previous night.

'Where are the children?' the snatcher said. 'You tell us or I will see they throw your friend Greta into jail.'

Petra looked at Greta, who winked back at her.

'Tell me,' the snatcher shouted. 'Tell me where the children are.'

'They are long gone,' Greta said, spitting blood onto the cobblestones. 'You will never find them.'

The snatcher turned and drew his sword. 'You speak again and I will run you through.'

With blood-soaked teeth, Greta smiled up at him. 'Such a big man with his little weapon.'

The man raised his sword and aimed it at Greta. Petra ran forward and grabbed the snatcher's arm. The snatcher swung his other arm and slammed his hand into her stomach. Petra doubled over and fell to her knees.

'Enough!' Peter's thundering voice cut through Petra's pain. She heard a boot knocking the wind out of someone's chest. 'Or I will throw you into jail myself.'

Petra felt hands gently rolling her over. She caught a glimpse of the snatcher running off into the distance.

'Are you OK?' Nat said, looking down with worried eyes.

'Nat,' Petra said, holding her stomach.

Something sparked in Nat's eyes. 'We need to get her home, Peter. We need to get her home immediately.'

Peter barked orders at the two guards. Hands lifted Petra to her feet.

'Can you walk?' Peter said.

'I think so,' Petra said, taking a step forward.

The guards stood on either side of Petra as they walked along the eastern wall. The eastern gate rose high in front of them. Nat and Peter spoke in hushed whispers behind her. Suddenly, she felt a cry escape from her. She doubled over and held her stomach.

Nat ran up and crouched. 'We need to take you to a doctor.'

'No,' Petra hissed into Nat's ear. 'The doctor will find out about the baby.'

'You could lose the baby if we don't get to a doctor,' Nat whispered.

'Just get me home, Nat,' Petra said, pulling herself up.

Nat turned to Peter. 'Can we get off the main road?'

'We can go through the trading district,' Peter said, turning north.

'Hold on to her elbows,' Nat said to the guards. 'Don't let her fall again.'

They wound through the streets of the quiet trading district. A while later, they walked out behind the town hall.

'How you doing?' Peter said, walking alongside Petra. 'You have us a bit scared here.'

'Better,' Petra said. 'I think Nat and I can manage from here.'

'I will send these two with you,' Peter said, waving his hand at the two guards.

'That is OK,' Petra said, shaking her head. 'I am safe in the northern district. I would like some alone time with Nat.'

'We will be fine, Peter,' Nat said.

Peter inclined his head, signalled to the guards, then moved away.

'Are you sure you are OK?' Nat said, as they started up the hill.

Petra gave Nat a weak smile. Her face, now white, showed strains from the pain.

'Let's get you home,' Nat said, linking her arm to Petra's.

'What the hell happened?' Ernest said. 'And why have you not called a doctor?'

Nat scuttled out of Petra's quarters.

'Well?' Ernest said, walking in and sitting on her bed. 'What is going on?'

Petra turned her head and stared out of the window.

Ernest took his daughter's hand in his own. 'Please tell me what is going on. First someone injured Harold, now you are not well.'

'How is Harold?' Petra said, looking back at her father.

'He is doing fine,' Ernest said. 'Now tell me what is happening.'

'Who is Donte, Father?' Petra said, meeting her father's eyes.

'What do you mean?' Ernest said, frowning.

'You heard me,' Petra said. 'Who is Donte, really?'

'He is a noble from the City of Lynn,' Ernest said. 'We have had this conversation already.'

'What businesses does he run?' Petra said. 'I heard a child snatcher say his name.'

Ernest snorted. 'I have no idea what you are talking about. What is a child snatcher?'

Petra thought for a moment. 'Did you know about the girls living in the alleys?'

'Is that what this is all about?' Ernest said, dropping Petra's hand. 'All this trouble because of children living in the alleys?'

'Abandoned girls, Father,' Petra said, her voice raising. 'No boys. Just abandoned girls!'

Ernest stood and paced around Petra's room. 'What do you care about these outcasts? You know the deal. I saved your mother from the alleys.'

'You saved one girl, Papa,' Petra said. 'Just one girl. The rest are living in the alleys. Starving, freezing, no clothes and with no hope whatsoever.'

'I still don't understand why this is bothering you so much,' Ernest said.

Petra turned her head and stared out of the window.

Ernest stopped pacing. He dropped his head into his hands. 'You are with child, aren't you?'

Petra ignored him.

'Look at me, Petra,' Ernest said.

Petra turned and looked at her father.

'Hargreaves?' Ernest said.

'Yes,' Petra said. 'But after what just happened, I don't know if the baby survived.'

Ernest sat back next to her and took her hand. 'This changes everything.'

'You are not angry?' Petra said, her eyebrows raising.

'This does jeopardise everything we have worked for,' Ernest said. 'But that is my grandchild you have there.'

'Oh, Papa,' Petra said, throwing her arms over her father. 'I thought you were going to demand I get rid of the baby.'

Ernest hugged Petra hard, then pulled away. 'I would never ask you to do such a thing. We need to get a doctor to examine you.'

'Will the doctor keep it quiet?' Petra said.

'He will,' Ernest said. 'What are you going to do now?'

'I would like to marry Hargreaves,' Petra said suddenly. 'I love him with everything.'

A long sigh escaped Ernest's lips. 'I thought you might say that.'

'It's a problem?' Petra said, dropping her gaze to her hands.

'Donte,' Ernest said. 'He will not take kindly to this.'

'I have a bad feeling about Donte,' Petra said. 'The child snatchers mentioned him by name. They said they would be in a lot of trouble if they didn't catch any children.'

'I think it has something to do with his cleaning service,' Ernest said. 'I saw a lot of girls cleaning the streets in the City of Lynn.'

'So he is using the girls as slaves?' Petra said.

Ernest shrugged. 'I am not sure if he is paying them.'

'The girls in the alleys are petrified of the snatchers,' Petra said. 'It is why I want them out of there.'

'And how do you propose to do that?' Ernest said.

'I tried to buy the old school in the weaving district, but they wouldn't let me. I gave my money to Harold so he could buy it,' Petra said. 'We are going to turn it into an inn but secretly create an orphanage for the children.'

A wide grin stretched over Ernest's face. A second later, he threw his head back and laughed.

'What?' Petra said, a smile creeping over her face.

'You are exactly like your mother,' Ernest said, leaning in and kissing Petra on the forehead. 'Of course you are creating an orphanage for the children. How silly of me to not figure it out.'

Petra grinned. 'I think Mama would have been proud.'

'Oh, she certainly would have,' Ernest said.

'I don't like the way this town and its men treat women, Papa. The way they just dump girls is barbaric.'

'I agree, but it is a City of Lynn rule,' Ernest said. 'It wasn't always this way. But something changed in the city many seasons ago.'

Petra leant back onto her pillow and placed a hand on her belly. 'Do you think I can marry Hargreaves?'

'You cannot,' Ernest said, a grim look appearing on his face. 'Unless Donte releases you from my promise. And that I cannot promise.'

'What do we have to do to get him to agree?' Petra said.

Ernest stood up. 'I need to think. Right now, though, the only thing we can do is ask.'

'What if he refuses?' Petra said.

With a glance at Petra's belly, Ernest rubbed his forehead. 'That, I don't think, is an option. He will demand you get rid of the child.'

'That will never happen,' Petra said.

Ernest moved to the top of the bed and rearranged Petra's pillows. 'Don't worry about that now. I will send for the doctor.'

Petra let out a long sigh. 'Thank you, Papa.'

Ernest kissed the top of Petra's head. 'Rest now.'

'Can you call Nat for me?' Petra said. 'I think she must be worried sick.'

'No need,' Ernest said, walking up to the door and yanking it open. 'She has been eavesdropping all along.'

Nat jumped and let out a yell. 'I am sorry, sir.'

Ernest chuckled. 'I know you too well, child. Petra needs you now.'

'Yes, sir,' Nat said, walking into the room.

Petra waited for her father to close the door. 'What did you hear?'

'Most of it,' Nat said, smiling. 'I am surprised at how your father reacted.'

'So was I, at first,' Petra said. 'Then I remembered my mother. She has had a good effect on him.'

'How are you feeling?' Nat said.

'I am OK,' Petra said. 'The pain is gone.'

'That is good to hear. So what's the plan?' Nat said. 'What will we do with the inn?'

'We continue as per plan,' Petra said, a look of determination appearing on her face. 'We transform it into an inn but use it to look after the children.'

'At least you won't have to hide from your father,' Nat said.

'I think he will help us,' Petra said.

'All we have to do now is deal with Donte?' Nat said.

Petra looked up at the ceiling. 'I have a bad feeling about him, Nat. A feeling that he is not going away.'

'So do I,' Nat said. 'I will get some of the people I know to look into him.'

'Don't get yourself into trouble,' Petra said. 'You have enough on your plate dealing with Peter and Leonard.'

Nat smiled. 'There is nothing to deal with. I am with Leonard now and that is how it is going to stay.'

Petra closed her eyes.

'I will see you tomorrow,' Nat said, moving to the door. 'Use the bell to call me if you need anything.'

Petra hummed a goodnight, then promptly fell asleep.

CHAPTER 5
OH NO, PLEASE, NO

Petra jumped at the harsh knock on her bedroom door.

'Who is it?'

'It's me – Nat – with the doctor,' Nat said through the door.

Petra sat up. 'Come in.'

Nat entered, then waved the doctor in. The skinny doctor walked up to the side of Petra's bed. He dropped a small bag onto the floor. 'May I?' he said, pointing at Petra's stomach.

Petra removed the covers.

The doctor pushed around her abdomen. 'Does it hurt?'

'No,' Petra said. 'The pain stopped last night.'

The doctor bent over, picked up his bag, then walked to the door. 'You will be fine.'

'Shouldn't you do more tests?' Nat said to an empty doorway.

'It's OK, Nat,' Petra said. 'He knows I am not wed. He wants nothing to do with me.'

Nat walked to the door and closed it a little too firmly. She walked over to Petra's bed and sat on the side. 'Someone else is here to see you.'

'Who?' Petra said, fear stretching across her face.

'Hargreaves,' Nat said.

'Oh,' Petra said. 'I thought you were going to say Donte.'

'Donte, I hear, is back in the City of Lynn,' Nat said. 'Something is happening in the north. He rushed off yesterday.'

Petra dropped her head onto her pillow and let out a sigh of relief.

'Would you like to see Hargreaves?' Nat said.

'I want to marry him, Nat,' Petra said as she stared at the ceiling.

'You want to do what?' Nat said, her eyebrows shooting into her hair.

'I want to marry Hargreaves,' Petra said.

'What about Donte and being a noble?' Nat said.

Petra lifted her head and gave Nat a smile. 'Everything has changed now I am carrying his baby. It is all very clear to me. He was the man I should have married all along.'

Nat stared at Petra with her mouth open.

'What?' Petra said, reaching over and grabbing Nat's hand.

'Your whole family have been aiming to achieve nobility,' Nat said. 'You have the chance and you have changed your mind? Have you told your father?'

'Didn't you hear us talking about it yesterday? I have told him,' Petra said. 'I thought he would be angry. But he is supporting my decision.'

'Definitely Hargreaves's lucky day then,' Nat said, a wide grin spreading across her face. 'How do you think he is going to react?'

'I don't know, but I will find out soon enough,' Petra said. 'What is happening with you and Leonard?'

Nat's cheeks turned a slight pink. 'We have set a date for the wedding.'

Petra squeezed Nat's hand. 'When? Tell me? We need to start preparations.'

'We are sticking with the first day of spring,' Nat said. 'You should be able to attend, shouldn't you?'

'I will be heavily pregnant, but don't you worry, nothing will keep me away from your wedding.'

Nat reached over and hugged Petra. 'I am so happy.'

'What about Peter?' Petra said.

'We spoke,' Nat said, pulling away. 'He is heartbroken, but he has promised me he will be OK.'

'Peter will be OK,' Petra said. 'The captain of Fairacre will have a lot of girls to choose from.'

'I think we will be friends one day,' Nat said. 'Now it's still a bit raw.'

'Time for me to see Hargreaves,' Petra said. 'Help me get out of this bed, will you?'

'Are you sure getting out of bed is a good idea?' Nat said. 'You have a baby to worry about.'

'I am fine,' Petra said. 'Just bruised.'

Petra climbed out of bed and winced at the stiffness in her body. A minute later, and after a few stretches, she was moving around her room freely. After dressing in the clothes Nat had left her, she left her quarters and walked down the stairs.

'They are in the trades room,' Nat said.

Petra walked up to the large double doors and knocked.

'Come,' Ernest said.

The doors swung open with the gentlest of pushes. Petra smiled at Hargreaves, who sat nervously with his hands in his lap.

'Petra,' Ernest said, walking around his desk and up to his daughter. 'I have been called to the City of Lynn. I am leaving today.'

'Oh,' Petra said. 'How long will you be gone for?'

'I am uncertain,' Ernest said. 'Dr Viktor has summoned me. I will leave you two alone. Call me within the next hour if you need me.'

'I will,' Petra said, then waited for the trading room doors to close.

'Why have I been called here, Petra?' Hargreaves said, standing up.

'Please sit,' Petra said, sitting next to Hargreaves.

Hargreaves sat and looked down at his hands.

'I have decided not to marry Donte.'

'What?' Hargreaves said, jerking his head up.

'I am not marrying Donte. I want to marry you.'

Hargreaves smiled broadly for a second, then his face sank.

'What's wrong?' Petra said, reaching over and holding Hargreaves's hand.

Hargreaves looked away. 'Donte is not going to like this, Petra. He is a dangerous man.'

'What do you mean?'

'There is a lot you don't know about him,' Hargreaves said. 'I was just explaining everything to your father.'

'Are you saying you don't want to marry me?' Petra said.

Hargreaves's head jerked up again. 'What?'

One of Petra's eyebrows popped up. 'I think you heard me.'

'What?' Hargreaves said.

Petra looked up at the ceiling and blew out a long breath that rattled her lips. She looked back at Hargreaves. 'Are you saying you don't want to marry me? I mean, it is the man's job to ask, so I don't know why I am doing it?'

Hargreaves slid off the chair and knelt in front of Petra. 'What has changed your mind? Why do you want me to marry you?'

Petra placed a hand on her belly and grinned.

'What?' Hargreaves said.

'Really?' Petra said, her voice rising. 'I am pregnant with your child, Hargreaves.'

Hargreaves sat on his heels and stared at Petra's belly. A moment later, he shook his head. 'Oh no. Oh no, please, no.'

Petra's breath caught in her throat. 'I thought you would be pleased?'

'I am pleased,' Hargreaves said, sitting up and taking Petra's hands.

'Then why don't I understand?' Petra said.

A tear trickled down Hargreaves's face.

'What is wrong?' Petra said, sliding off the chair and wrapping her arms around Hargreaves's neck.

'Donte,' Hargreaves whispered. 'He won't allow you to keep the child.'

Petra leant back and frowned. 'Donte has no say on whether we keep the child, Hargreaves.'

'He does,' Hargreaves said. 'Your father promised you would marry him.'

'He will understand,' Petra said. 'My father will help. Everything will be OK.'

Hargreaves dropped his head onto Petra's shoulder.

'Come on,' Petra said, rising and pulling Hargreaves up. 'We have a lot to get done before the winter gets here.'

Hargreaves squared his shoulders and took in a deep breath. 'Petra, if we can, will you marry me?'

Petra threw her arms over Hargreaves's shoulders. 'Of course I will.'

'That's settled then,' Hargreaves said into her shoulder. 'We will have to deal with Donte somehow.'

'I love the smell of autumn,' Nat said.

The sound of hammering filled the bottom end of the weaving district. Petra stood outside the front door and cast a critical eye over the new entrance to the inn. Men walked in and out of the double doors carrying building materials and tools.

'It is starting to take shape,' Nat said.

'We have replaced most of the rotting floor and the stairs,' Petra said. 'It will be safe for us to enter in another few weeks.'

Nat cast her eyes to the sky. 'I can feel the autumn creeping in.'

'The air has a slight chill,' Petra said, pulling the cloak tighter around herself.

'What would Harold like done with all the broken internal doors, ma'am?' a man said, walking out of the double doors.

'You can get rid of them,' Petra said. 'Harold will be replacing all the internal doors.'

'As you wish,' the man said, with a slight bow.

'I see the men are only answering to Harold still,' Nat said.

'I don't care right now,' Petra said. 'I want to get these girls off the streets, and I will do everything in my power to make it happen.'

'Any news from Donte?' Nat said.

Petra shook her head. 'Hargreaves is getting agitated about the whole thing. He wants to tell Donte and get it over and done with.'

'I am sure Donte will be back soon,' Nat said.

'My father thinks there is something really bad happening north of the City of Lynn,' Petra said. 'He doesn't think Donte will be back before the spring.'

'Will your father be going to the City of Lynn?' Nat said.

'I don't think so,' Petra said. 'He caused a bit too much trouble the last time he was there.'

A cloud passed overhead and blocked out the sun. Nat shivered.

'Autumn is definitely here,' Petra said.

'I always loved winter,' Petra said, wrapping her arms around herself.

The wind battered the front door of the recently painted inn.

'It's absolutely freezing,' Harold said. 'Please come inside, my lady. I wouldn't want you to catch a cold.'

'You are my Grandpapa,' Petra said, curling a hand over Harold's forearm. 'You don't need to call me my lady.'

Harold smiled down at his granddaughter. 'The men finished the kitchens this morning. I don't think we'll have a problem feeding a lot of people.'

'We should be close to finishing the entire inn by the time spring arrives,' Petra said.

'The rooms at the back are just about complete,' Harold said, his voice lowering.

Petra looked from side to side. 'When can we start getting these children off the streets?'

'Greta and the girls are working out a schedule,' Harold said. 'We need to do it quietly.'

'As long as they know they still need to be seen in the alleys during the day,' Petra said.

Harold wrapped his arm around his granddaughter. 'They are putting together a rota.'

The inn's front door banged open. 'What are you doing out in this cold?' Nat shouted. 'You have a baby inside of you. Get in here right this minute.'

'Yes ma'am,' Petra said, walking up the stairs. 'Anything else, ma'am?'

Harold chuckled as he followed her up the stairs.

With one hand on her hip, Nat tapped her foot as Petra and Harold walked through the door.

'So dramatic,' Petra said.

The inn door slammed shut.

'I have news,' Nat said. 'Leonard and I have set a date.'

Petra hugged her. 'That is fantastic news. When?'

'The first Sunday of spring,' Nat said.

'Congratulations, Natalie,' Harold said.

'I want you to give me away, Harold,' Nat said over Petra's shoulder.

He stared at her.

'And I want you to be my maid of honour,' Nat said, pulling away from Petra.

'I thought you would never ask,' Petra said with a small curtsy.

'I am not your father,' Harold said matter-of-factly.

Nat smiled up at Harold. 'You have always been my father, Harold. Please, will you give me away?'

'I will,' Harold said, his voice cracking. 'It will be my honour.'

'You do know I will be massive,' Petra said, looking down at her belly. 'I am already starting to show a bit.'

'It is why we are having our wedding as soon as spring arrives,' Nat said. 'I couldn't bear having my wedding without you there. You might not have wanted to come with a newborn.'

'We are done with the upstairs, my lady,' a man said, double-stepping down the newly built staircase.

'What else needs to be done?' Petra said.

'The dining room and then we are done,' the man said. 'We will finish in two weeks.'

'Ahead of time, then,' Petra said.

'We need to move the grand opening, my lady,' Harold said. 'We can do it before spring arrives.'

'A grand opening,' Nat said, spreading her arms dramatically. 'Fairacre's first-ever inn, book now.'

'Aren't we supposed to be keeping this quiet?' Petra said.

'I think Nat is right,' Harold said. 'We need to plan a grand opening and make sure everyone sees this place as an inn. That way they see us as not hiding anything.'

'I will have to think of a guest list then,' Petra said. 'We can invite the traders from the northern district.'

'And the owners in the entertainment district,' Harold said.

'We need to speak to Peter about security,' Nat said. 'I can do that.'

Petra tilted her head. 'How is it going between the two of you?'

'I want us to be friends,' Nat said. 'Best way to do that is to get him involved.'

'Tread carefully, Natalie,' Harold said. 'He will need time.'

Nat headed for the door. 'I will see you back at the house where we can plan.'

Petra waited for the front door to close. 'Follow me,' she said, beckoning Harold.

They walked into the kitchen and to a small door on the back wall.

Petra opened the door to reveal a pantry. She reached up to the highest shelf and clicked a button. The left shelves moved to the side, revealing a staircase. 'It goes up to the rows of rooms for the girls. Would you like to see?'

'Of course,' Harold said. 'I want to look it over.'

They walked up the staircase and onto the narrow landing. Harold moved down the thin corridor until he reached a door, which he opened. Inside the room, on each wall, sat three bunk beds, one on top of the other.

'We can sleep nine girls, maybe twelve, in each room,' Petra said. 'We have eight rooms, so about seventy girls.'

Harold walked into the room and scanned the bunks. 'I would hate to live in a cramped place like this.'

'It is a lot better than sleeping in the alleys,' Petra said. 'They will be warm and dry in here.'

'That they will,' Harold said, gripping the bunk bed and shaking it. 'How will the girls escape if they have to?'

'Out of the windows and onto the next roof,' Petra said, leading her grandfather out of the dormitory and up to a window. 'You see how you can jump over this alley?'

Harold rubbed his chin. 'You need to get them to practise the jump. It is quite far.'

'Way ahead of you, Grandpapa,' Petra said with a grin. 'Greta has been showing the young girls what to do.'

Harold's face broke into a smile. 'Of course you have this all in hand. How else can the girls get in here?'

'That's it,' Petra said. 'The staircase up through the pantry, or through the windows and onto the rooftops.'

Harold thought for a moment. 'Then it is very important they learn how to get through these windows quickly.'

'It's time to get back home,' Petra said, heading for the staircase. 'Papa is waiting for me and we need to continue planning the grand opening.'

'Nat, Harold, it's time to get moving,' Petra shouted.

'The sun isn't even up yet,' Nat grumbled as she walked down the staircase. 'And there has been a fresh fall of snow.'

The front door banged open. Harold stepped into the house and stamped his feet on the ground. 'Not too sure how many people will turn up in this weather. It's very cold.'

'It should be warmer by the time we open the inn,' Petra said. 'Let's get moving.'

'Wait,' Nat said, standing in front of Petra with a thick woollen cloak. 'You know the drill.'

Petra rolled her eyes but grinned. She extended her arm and

slipped on the heavy cloak. The belt tightened around her expanding belly.

'Ready?' Harold said, opening the door.

Petra sucked in a quick breath as the cold air slammed into her face. She dropped her head and walked out into the twilight morning.

'Crazy,' Nat said. 'This is crazy weather.'

Harold chuckled. 'You have been living in that mansion for too long, my dear.'

Petra and Nat linked arms with Harold as they walked down the hill towards the centre of Fairacre. The road this early in the morning lay empty apart from the men who shovelled the snow off the pavement. They entered the town square and waited at the south-eastern corner.

'Good morning,' Greta said. 'Lovely day for an inn opening, isn't it?'

'Crazy,' Nat muttered, pulling the collar of her cloak over her mouth. 'We should be indoors next to a fireplace.'

'Come on, Natalie,' Harold said, wrapping his arm around her. 'When we get to the inn, you can warm up.'

They continued down the southern road and into the weaving district. The alleys lay cold and empty.

'Are all the girls in the inn, Greta?' Petra said quietly.

'They are,' Greta said. 'Half of them will be leaving now for the alleys. It's been hard to make them realise why they have to go back.'

'But they are doing it?' Petra said, raising both eyebrows.

'Yes,' Greta said. 'They understand they have to make the town believe they are still in the alleys.'

'And if they don't, they will shut us down and the girls will lose their beds?' Petra said.

'They know how important it is, my lady,' Greta said.

They continued past the arts and crafts shop. The southern wall loomed up in front of them. They turned left and continued along the wall until the new inn came into view.

'You should be proud,' Harold said, stopping at the bottom of the inn's steps. 'It looks brand new compared to the rest of the buildings in the weaving district.'

'I couldn't have done it without all of you,' Petra said, hugging Harold. 'Come on. We have a lot to do before midday.'

The front doors swung open without a sound. The entrance hall smelled of new wood varnish. In every corner stood a large brass vase, ready for umbrellas and walking sticks. In the summer, they would fill them with an abundance of flowers.

'I will get the fires going in the kitchen,' Harold said.

'We have some cleaning to do,' Nat said, grabbing Greta by the arm. 'And some rooms to get ready.'

Petra led Harold into the kitchen and through the small door into the pantry. She clicked the button and moved the shelves. In single file, they walked up the narrow staircase. The whispers of children's voices fell silent as they shushed each other. Petra walked onto the landing and up to the first door.

'Open up,' Petra said, giving the secret knock.

The door swung open. Wide eyes stared at her from the bunks lining the walls.

'Miss Petra,' Harriet said, jumping off the bunk and running over. 'Do you like our room?'

'It's looking great,' Petra said. 'Are you all nice and warm?'

Smiles beamed back at Petra as all the kids nodded together.

'Where is Fay?' Petra said.

'She has gone to the alleys,' Harriet said. 'She will make some noise, so everyone thinks we are still living there.'

'Good,' Petra said. 'And when it is your turn, you will need to make noise too.'

The girls nodded back.

Petra, followed by Harriet and Harold, went from door to door to check on the rest of the girls. She shook her head at the sorry state of some of the frailer children. Red sores blistered and bled on their knees and elbows. Each one, though, smiled back as they sat in their new, warm rooms.

'There is going to be a lot of noise downstairs today,' Petra said. 'You all need to keep very quiet.'

'I will make sure,' Harriet said, lifting her chin and folding her arms. 'I will tell them.'

'And you know how to escape if you need to, Harriet?' Harold said.

'Yes, mister,' Harriet said. 'Through the windows and across the roof.'

'Excellent,' Petra said, clapping her hands. 'We need to go and get ready now.'

Harriet followed Petra to the stairs, then wrapped her arms around her legs. 'Thank you for our new home.'

Petra rubbed Harriet's back. 'You are welcome. Now remember to behave and keep quiet.'

Harriet grinned up at her, then ran back into her room. Petra chuckled as she shushed the rest of the girls.

Petra and Harold walked down the stairs, through the pantry door, and into the kitchen.

Harold walked from stove to stove, where he poked and prodded the coals until they shone a bright yellow.

Petra warmed her hands over one of the stoves. 'I will get the food going in a second.'

'As long as you let me carry the heavy things,' Harold said, glancing at her belly.

'You are going to be a great-grandpapa soon,' Petra said, walking over to hug him.

'Makes me feel old,' Harold said.

'Let's get the food on the go,' Petra said.

They warmed up the foodstuff for the guests' lunch. About fifteen minutes before noon, they took the large trays of food into the dining room. Once the tables were full, Petra made her way to the entrance hall, where she checked herself in the mirror.

'Your little one is getting bigger,' Greta said, as she dusted the top of the mirror.

'A few more months,' Petra said.

'It's time,' Nat said, walking up to the front door. 'Harold, as the owner of the inn, can you lead the way?'

'Certainly,' Harold said, moving over to the front door.

Petra walked over to the coat stand and pulled her large cloak around her. She walked to the front door and stood next to Harold. The door flew open.

'Oh my,' Petra said, walking onto the top step. 'This is unexpected.'

'Very unexpected,' Harold said.

'Please come in,' Nat said, waving to the first trader. 'Welcome to the inn.'

Harold shook the trader's hand as he entered the inn. Petra curtsied. One by one, the traders shook Harold's hand, bowed and walked into the entrance hall. Nat took their coats and directed them into the dining room.

'The queue goes around to the arts and crafts shop,' Harold said.

'Do you think we have enough space?' Petra said, curtsying to another trader.

'I am sure we will be OK,' Harold said. 'Hello, Peter.'

'Hello, Harold, Petra,' Peter said.

'Hi, Peter,' Nat said from the coat stand.

'Natalie,' Peter said, walking over. 'This is such an achievement by all of you. The inn looks fantastic.'

'Thank you,' Nat said with a smile.

Peter walked into the dining room.

'Nat, come over here. Your future husband has arrived,' Petra said. 'He is smiling from ear to ear.'

Nat skipped over to the entrance and hugged Leonard. 'I will join you when I can.'

Leonard extended his hand to Harold. 'It is an honour to be part of the first inn ever built in Fairacre. Very well done.'

Harold nodded. 'Thank you, Leonard. We couldn't have done it without you.'

Leonard blushed a dark red.

It took another thirty minutes for the rest of the guests to walk through the front door. Petra closed the doors, hung up her cloak, and made her way into the dining room. Nat beckoned her over to the head of the table.

'It's so loud,' Petra said into Nat's ear.

'I think you can agree this opening is a success,' Nat said.

'Where is Hargreaves?' Petra said. 'I didn't see him come in.'

Nat frowned. 'I haven't either.'

'Would you like me to look for him?' Harold said.

Petra shook her head. 'No, you cannot leave. You are the owner of this inn.'

'I think you need to walk around the room, Harold,' Nat said. 'There are a lot of people waiting for you.'

Harold looked at Nat with wide eyes. 'You didn't tell me I would have to do that.'

'I will come with you,' Petra said. 'The traders know us.'

Harold and Petra made their way around the dining room. They shook hands and spoke to each of the guests. An hour later, they made it around to where they had started.

'Hargreaves has just arrived,' Nat said, signalling to the door.

Petra frowned at the dark bags under Hargreaves's eyes. 'What is wrong with him?'

Hargreaves walked up and grabbed Petra's hands. 'I am sorry I am late.'

'What is wrong?' Petra said. 'You look terrible. Are you OK?'

'Donte,' Hargreaves said. 'He arrived this morning.'

Petra took in a deep breath. 'Then I shall speak to him today and tell him I am marrying you.'

The inn's front doors slammed open. A large man with sparkling jewels in his hand strode into the dining room. He looked at Hargreaves and snarled.

'Take a step back, my lady,' Harold said, pulling Petra behind him.

'I am not hiding, Grandpapa,' Petra said, moving forward.

The room fell silent as Donte walked up to Petra.

'Good day, Donte,' Petra said, holding out her hand.

'You have embarrassed me,' Donte said, his face contorted in anger. 'Nobody ever embarrasses me.'

'I am sorry you feel that way,' Petra said. 'But I have decided to marry Hargreaves.'

'Your father promised you to me,' Donte said. 'I demand you get rid of this bastard child and marry me.'

Petra wrapped her hands around her belly. 'I am marrying Hargreaves. I am having this child and I am keeping it.'

Donte took a step forward.

Harold's large hand shot forward and slammed into Donte's chest. 'Step back, sir.'

'Take a step back, sir,' Peter said, stepping next to Harold. 'We will not have anyone destroy this grand opening.'

With a snarl, Donte swiped Harold's hand away. 'I will speak to your father about this.'

Petra remained quiet.

Donte scanned the room, turned and strode to the front door. A large man with a thick moustache smirked back at Petra. The doors slammed closed as Donte left.

Murmurs trickled through the guests.

'Harold, we need to sort the guests out,' Nat said.

'I will help,' Leonard said.

Harold and Leonard moved into the throng.

'Are you OK?' Nat said, wrapping her arm around Petra.

Petra nodded. 'I am fine.'

'I am sorry,' Hargreaves said. 'I am sorry, Petra, but I cannot marry you.'

'What?' Petra said, grabbing Hargreaves by the arm. 'What do you mean?'

Hargreaves pulled his arm away and walked towards the front door.

'Come back here, Hargreaves,' Petra said, taking a step forward.

'Let him go, Petra,' Nat said. 'You cannot go out there with Donte back in town.'

'I will speak to him,' Peter said. 'Make sure you stay at the inn. That thug with the moustache looks dangerous.'

Petra stared at the front door as Peter walked through. 'I don't understand, Nat. What is going on?'

'I don't know,' Nat said.

Petra pulled her shoulders back and placed a smile on her face. She turned and made her way over to Harold.

CHAPTER 6
COME ON, HARRIET

'Can I come in?' Nat said from the other side of the door. 'It's been nearly a week, Petra. You cannot hide forever.'

Petra spun in her bed so her back was to the door. The sunrise sent a ray of light through her bedroom windows. The snow had just about melted.

'Petra, please can I come in?' Nat said. 'We need to talk.'

'Go away,' Petra said into her pillow.

The door rattled. 'Petra, this is your grandpapa. It is important you let us in.'

Petra sat up and sighed. 'What do you want?'

'Let us in,' Nat said. 'Or I will get Harold to break down this door.'

'OK, OK, OK,' Petra mumbled as she threw her legs over the side of the bed. 'I am coming.'

The lock turned and clicked. Petra pulled open the door, then walked back to her bed. Nat walked up to the window and pulled the curtains closed. Harold shut the door, then stood in front of it with his arms folded.

'How is the baby?' Nat said, walking around the bed.

'Fine,' Petra said, cradling her belly. 'Kicking hard but everything is fine. What is so urgent?'

Nat sat on the bed next to Petra. 'It's Donte. Peter says he has become very agitated over the last few days.'

'I couldn't care less about Donte or Hargreaves,' Petra said, folding her arms. 'They can both rot in hell.'

Harold cleared his throat and raised an eyebrow.

'Donte has sent a message,' Nat whispered.

Petra frowned. 'And?'

'He is demanding you still marry him,' Nat said. 'He said you can give the baby to someone who will look after it.'

Petra stood and balled her fists by her side. 'I am not giving up my child, Nat.'

'Donte said he will destroy you, your father and Harold's inn, if you don't do what he says.'

'He wouldn't?' Petra said, her shoulders slumping. 'He wouldn't destroy my father.'

A loud banging came from downstairs.

'Wait here,' Harold said, turning. He opened the door.

The banging grew louder.

Nat walked over to the door and held it open just a crack.

'Where is she?' Peter shouted.

Swinging open the door, Nat said, 'What is it Peter?'

Peter's footsteps echoed through the house as he double-stepped up the stairs. He stopped at the bedroom's entrance and surveyed the room.

'You are scaring me, Peter,' Nat said. 'What is going on?'

'Donte is sending his thugs to fetch Petra,' Peter said. 'We need to get you out of here.'

'I am not afraid of him, Peter,' Petra said.

'You should be,' he said, striding over to the window. 'He will

95

enslave you and your newborn child. We need to get you out of here. And we need to do it now.'

'You need to listen to Peter,' Harold said. 'I don't think I can protect you from all of them.'

Petra looked at Nat, who gave her a single nod.

'OK,' Petra said. 'Where do you suggest we go?'

Peter scratched the side of his head. 'That is the issue. I don't know. The town hall with Hargreaves would be safest.'

'I don't trust him,' Petra said, folding her arms.

The front door rattled.

'They are here,' Peter whispered. 'We need to go.'

'Where, though?' Nat said.

Peter looked out of the window again and pointed to the wall. 'The alleys are an option.'

Petra froze, and then she turned to Harold. 'We need to get the children from the inn. Harold, we need to get the girls.'

'They will be expecting that,' Peter said. 'We need to stay away from the inn.'

'We are going to the inn,' Petra said, her voice lowering to a growl. 'Let's go through the alleys.'

'My lady,' Harold said, waving his hand at the stairs. 'We need to go out the back and through the gate to the wall.'

'I will lead,' Peter said. 'Through the alleys towards the inn.'

Petra, Nat and Harold followed Peter down the stairs. The pounding on the front door rattled through the house. Peter headed for the back door, shadowed by the others. They looked on as he held up his hand and tilted his head.

'Can you hear anything?' Nat whispered.

Peter shook his head, then opened the door. He stepped out into the morning sunlight. 'It's clear. Harold, can you bring up the rear?'

Harold pulled the hood of his cloak over his head then clicked his mask into place.

'Let's go,' Peter said, hurrying to the small gate.

Petra followed Nat and Peter through. They followed the fence to the wall and turned south. In the distance, a smash of glass echoed through the quiet morning.

'They have broken into the house,' Peter said over his shoulder. 'It will take them moments to see we are not there.'

Petra sucked in a gulp of air, then doubled over.

'Petra, are you OK?' Nat said, placing her hand on her back.

'There's a sharp pain in my belly,' Petra said. 'But I am OK, let's keep going.'

'Are you sure?' Peter said, dropping to a knee and looking at her. 'You have gone pale.'

'Keep going, please,' Petra said, straightening up. 'We cannot let those thugs catch us.'

They continued along the wall until the distant sounds of the entertainment district filtered through to them.

Peter slowed, then stopped. He walked back along the wall and frowned.

'What is it?' Nat said.

'Those sounds are the boots of guards running along the wall,' Peter said. 'They will be on top of us any minute.'

'Can we get to the entertainment district and move through the crowds?' Nat said.

Peter shook his head. 'They will capture us straight away.'

Harold cleared his throat. 'If I may, sir?'

'Please, Harold, no need to call me sir. What are you thinking?' Peter said.

'I suggest we get onto the rooftops,' Harold said, pointing up. 'It is where I usually keep an eye on my Petra.'

They all looked skywards at the same time.

'How do we get up there?' Petra said, her hand wrapping around her belly.

Harold walked up to a set of crates that sat on top of each other. Then he hauled them around until they made a crude staircase up to a thick ledge. He held out his hand to Nat.

'Where do I go from the top of the crates?' Nat said, grabbing his hand.

'Use those pipes to pull you up,' Harold said, pointing to a set of drainage pipes. 'Once you and Peter are up there, we will help Petra.'

Nat threw out her other hand to maintain her balance. The crates cracked and creaked but stayed whole. At the top, she grabbed the pipes and used the ledges until she disappeared onto the flat roof. Peter bounded up the crates and followed Nat onto the flat roof.

'You will be fine,' Harold said, smiling at Petra.

Petra held onto Harold's hand as she climbed up the crates. She stepped on a ledge and grabbed a drainpipe.

'We will help pull you up,' Peter said as he leant over the lip of the roof. 'Give me your hand.'

Petra threw up her hand, which Peter grabbed. 'Don't worry, I won't drop you.'

'Give me your other hand,' Nat said, leaning over the roof. 'You need to hurry. I can see the guards coming down the alley.'

Petra's knuckles turned white as she gripped Peter's and Nat's hands. She scrambled up the pipes until she reached the edge of the building. With one big pull, they dragged her over the ledge.

Harold scrambled up the crates. Hand over hand, he scaled the pipes and leapt onto the roof.

'I see you have done this before,' Peter said, panting.

'Get down here!' a guard shouted.

Harold picked up a plank and threw it at the guards. With yells, the guards ran back up the alley. Harold crouched next to the other three. 'Keep close and keep your head down,' he said, facing the south. 'We need to reach the southern gate to cross over to the weaving district.'

They walked as quickly as Petra could manage. At every alley, they balanced a plank over the gap and manoeuvred across.

'You have been busy, Harold,' Peter said, jumping off a plank. 'Is there one across every alley?'

Harold smiled. 'Yes, I can get around the whole of Fairacre from here.'

'Oh no,' Nat said, grabbing Peter's arm. 'Look over there.'

Petra gasped. 'Is that a fire?'

'It looks like it's coming from the inn,' Harold said.

'The children, Harold,' Petra said. 'They will burn in there.'

'Where are the children?' Peter said. 'How do I get to them?'

'If you stand on the opposite roof, they are in the rooms directly across,' Petra said.

Peter took off along the rooftops. Petra, Nat and Harold didn't bother crouching anymore. They moved south as quickly as possible.

'We will have to cross the north–south road,' Harold said. 'We can jump onto the southern wall and walk over the gate.'

At the southern wall, they followed Harold's lead.

'They are going to die,' Petra said, her breathing laboured. 'Those poor girls are going to die in there.'

'Peter will get them,' Nat said. 'He knows what he is doing, Petra.'

A few minutes later, they approached the opposite side of the inn. Shouts of people giving instructions sounded from the alley. Weaving district residents passed buckets along as they tried to put out the fire.

'Where is he?' Nat said, looking around wildly.

A window smashed. Smoke billowed out. A small girl climbed through, followed by another and another. Peter's head appeared through the smoke.

'Jump,' Harold said, holding out his arms.

The young girls stared in shock.

Peter jumped out of the window, grabbed the nearest girl, and threw her across the alley. Harold caught her in his massive arms. Peter threw the girls one at a time from the inn to the roof.

'How many are there?' Peter shouted.

'Twenty,' Petra shouted back. 'Including Harriet.'

Peter disappeared into the smoke. A few seconds later, more girls climbed out. One by one, Harold caught them.

Petra knelt and pulled the young girls together.

'Peter,' Nat shouted. 'Get out of there.'

A thick billow of smoke chugged out of the window, followed by a massive yellow flame.

'Peter?' Nat screamed. 'Where is he, Harold?'

'Peter?' Harold bellowed.

A second later, another window smashed open. Girls climbed out onto the ledges. Harold ran to the lip of the roof and stretched out his arms. One at a time, he pulled them onto the roof.

'Where is Harriet?' Petra said, doing a head count.

'Did you see Peter?' Nat asked one of the girls.

The girl shook her head and wiped the tears from her eyes. With a crash, another window shattered. Peter appeared on the ledge holding a small girl.

'Harriet,' Petra said. 'Is she OK, Peter?'

Harold ran over and took Harriet from him. He laid her on the ground and placed his head on her chest.

'Is she breathing?' Nat said.

Petra ran over and knelt. She grabbed Harriet's nose and blew a long breath into her lungs. 'Come on, Harriet.'

A second later, Harriet coughed. Petra sat back with a sigh of relief.

'Is she going to be OK?' Peter said, dropping to his knees next to them.

Petra pulled Harriet to a seating position and checked her bloodshot eyes. 'I think she will be OK.'

Nat knelt next to Peter and threw her arms around his neck. 'Are you OK?'

'Smoke in my lungs,' Peter said, coughing. 'And my eyes are stinging.'

'We need to move,' Harold said. 'They will be on the rooftops any second.'

'Where do we go?' Petra said.

'Follow me,' a girl said.

Petra swung around to see Fay's head poking over the rooftop.

'Where are we going?' Nat said, standing and rounding up the girls.

'No time,' Fay said. 'Follow me.'

Petra and Nat guided the girls to the roof's edge. Harold threw Peter's arm over his neck and pulled him along. Ledges and crates formed a staircase to the alley's floor. One by one, they made it to the bottom.

'Where to?' Petra said, squinting into the dark alley.

Fay walked over to a large grate. She grabbed it with both hands and pulled it out of its hole. 'We go to the sewers,' she said.

Water dripped from the ceiling. The droplets splashed into the water and echoed down the sewers. The girls stood in a long line, holding hands. Nat walked up and down the line with her finger on her lips.

'Do you know which way to go?' Petra said, kneeling in front of Fay.

'No, miss,' Fay said. 'I don't come down too often.'

'We need to walk west,' Harold said. 'The sewers extend past the town walls. Not many people know they exist.'

Peter started to cough violently.

'He needs to keep quiet, miss,' Fay said. 'You can hear everything from the alleys.'

'Let's throw caution to the wind,' Harold said. 'I will lead the way. Make sure everyone keeps up.'

Petra stayed at the front of the girls, while Nat stayed at the back. They followed Harold through the winding sewer tunnels until he brought them to a halt. He spun around and placed a finger on his lips.

Petra turned and shushed the girls.

'Get your men into the sewers,' a man shouted. 'I don't want to hear any complaints.'

The girls moved against the sewer wall. The older girls wrapped their arms around the younger ones. In the distance, the scraping of a sewer gate echoed through the tunnels.

'Move,' Harold said. 'They are nearby.'

They walked as quickly as they could through the tunnels. The girls remained quiet even when they fell over or bashed their legs. The guards' pounding boots drew closer and closer.

Nat brought the rear of the girls up to the front to bunch everyone together. 'They will be on us in a few minutes,' she said. 'I can hear their footsteps getting louder.'

Peter coughed loudly, then pulled Nat into a hug. 'Keep going,' he whispered into her ear.

'What are you doing, Peter?' Nat said.

'I will hold them off as long as I can,' he said. 'I cannot stop coughing and they are using me to track us. Keep going. I will lead them away.'

'Peter,' Nat said, taking a step forward. 'Don't do anything stupid, please.'

'Go.' He pushed Nat away and drew his sword. 'Get these girls to safety, Nat. Make sure you look after them.'

'Come on, Nat,' Petra said. 'We need you with us.'

Nat gave Peter a kiss on the cheek, then turned and followed her into the darkness. The group turned left, then right, then left again as they followed Harold's big frame. Eventually the tunnels narrowed. The water that ran along the tunnels disappeared.

'We are outside the town walls,' Harold said, over his shoulder. 'We need to find the old town.'

Petra hurried forward until she stood shoulder to shoulder with Harold. 'What old town?'

'Farmacre,' Harold said. 'We built Fairacre on top of it. The sewers run a long way past the town walls.'

The tunnel narrowed until Harold had to stoop to stop his head from hitting the ceiling. They suddenly hit a small room with tunnels leading in all directions.

'Which way?' Petra said.

Harold knelt. He turned in every direction and listened. 'I have no idea,' he said. 'I think we will have to guess.'

The sound of sword fighting echoed through the tunnels.

'Peter,' Nat said, quietly. 'They have found him.'

'Which way do we go, Nat?' Petra said, trying to distract her best friend.

Nat wiped a tear off her cheek. 'I think we should go north.'

Harold stood and moved through the northern tunnel. The bunched-up girls followed quietly.

'Wait a second, miss,' Fay said.

'What is it, Fay?' Petra said.

'We are leaving footsteps in the sand,' Fay said. 'I think we should cover them up.'

Harriet jumped from foot to foot.

'Yes, you can help,' Fay said.

Petra and the two girls dropped to their knees. With their hands, they rubbed the footsteps away. They slowly backed into the northern tunnel. Petra tapped the two girls on the shoulder and pointed forward to get them moving. They ran quietly to join the group. Petra tilted her head and listened. The sound of swords striking each other filled the tunnels. She turned and hurried after the train of girls.

'Did you hear him?' Nat said, as Petra reached the back of the train.

'He is still fighting,' Petra said. 'I think he is making them chase him.'

Nat bit her bottom lip. 'Is he going to die?'

'I am sure he will get away,' Petra said, wrapping her arm over Nat's shoulder.

'I have found something,' Harold said.

Petra and Nat hurried forward. The girls stood with their backs to the tunnel walls.

'What is it?' Petra said.

'It's a door,' Harold said. 'I found it by dragging my hand along the wall.'

Petra copied her grandfather's action until she felt the corner of an old metal door. She traced her fingers around the frame until she found the handle. It turned with a squeal, but the door didn't budge.

'Let me try,' Harold said, gripping the handle with both hands. With a grunt, he pushed hard. The door budged with a scrape. He pushed again. The door moved an inch. 'Can you see anything?' he said.

Petra closed one eye and peered inside. 'It's too dark. It looks like a room.'

Harold pushed again. Sweat streamed down his face.

'Let me look,' Fay said. 'I can get inside.'

'Will the door stay open?' Nat said.

Harold let go of the door. It stayed where he left it.

'OK, go inside, but take Harriet with you,' Petra said.

The two girls snaked their way through the crack and disappeared into the darkness. A second later, Fay's head popped through the gap. 'It's a lot of little rooms. We can hide in here.'

'Move back,' Harold said.

Fay's head disappeared.

Harold placed his full weight on the door and pushed. The door squealed open fully.

'They will hear that,' Nat said.

'Not if Peter has led them away,' Harold said. 'Everyone, get in as quickly as possible.'

Petra and Nat ushered the girls through the small opening. After everyone was inside, Harold placed his weight against the door until it squealed shut.

Quiet descended on the small room.

'Over here, miss,' Harriet whispered. 'There is a big room.'

The girls walked through the door Harriet had found.

'Look, miss. Ledges all around the room,' Harriet said. 'Like beds.'

The girls filed into the room and jumped onto the ledges. Petra and Nat sat on the ledge nearest the room with the door.

'What do we do now?' Nat said.

'We wait, we keep quiet, and we survive,' Petra said. 'Like disgusting, filthy sewer rats.'

'These girls are incredible,' Nat said, scanning the room. 'They have remained so quiet.'

'Years of living in the alleys,' Petra said. 'It's so sad they have had to live like this.'

'Shh,' Harold said, placing a finger on his lips.

Muffled footsteps sounded on the other side of the door. Voices echoed through the long tunnels.

Harriet lifted Petra's arm and snuggled into her armpit.

Nat leant in close. 'I think they have walked past.'

Petra smiled with a nod.

Her expression changed when an almighty bang hit the big metal door.

'I think they went in here.'

Harold walked calmly over to the door and placed his weight behind it.

'Help me push it open,' a man said.

Fay tiptoed up to Harold and placed herself against the door. One by one, the girls moved up to Harold and placed their hands on the door.

'Push,' the guard said.

The door remained closed.

'They would never be able to get in there,' the guard said. 'How are girls supposed to get that open?'

'One more try,' the guard said. 'One, two, three, push!'

Harold and the girls leant against the door. It stayed firmly shut.

'Let's go,' a guard said. 'They have moved further along the tunnels.'

The footsteps disappeared down the tunnel. Harold stayed with his weight against the door. The girls didn't move an inch. They waited with eyes firmly set on Harold. A minute later, he gave everyone a nod. The girls, one by one, moved away from the door and back into the large room.

'That was close,' Petra whispered.

'Very close,' Harold said. 'These young ladies helped save the day.'

Petra surveyed the room. The girls sat with their mouths shut, but their eyes were bright and wide.

'They have lost their home, but they still have each other,' Nat said.

'I think we have found a new home,' Petra said, standing up. 'Look around you. With a little work, we can sort this place out.'

Nat frowned. 'What do you mean? Live here? Only rats live down here in the sewers.'

'Exactly,' Petra said. 'Who would come and search for these girls when the only things living down here are rats?'

'We could train them,' Harold said. 'We could train them to look after themselves.'

Petra placed a hand on Harold's forearm. 'You would do that for us?'

'Of course, my lady,' Harold said with a smile.

'What will we need to get started?' Petra said.

Harold tapped his chin. 'We need to sort this place out. We need access to food and clothes. And finally, we need access to wooden weapons.'

'How will you get all that?' Nat said.

Both Petra and Harold turned and smiled at Nat.

'Oh, come on,' Nat said. 'How am I going to get all that?'

'We will help, miss,' Fay said. 'We can find food and material.'

A few more girls jumped off the ledges. 'We can help clean this place as well.'

A smile spread across Petra's face. 'Look at all of you wanting to help create your new home. I am so proud of you.'

'It's still a place where only rats should live,' Nat said.

'Squeak, squeak, I am a sewer rat,' Harriet said.

'Squeak, squeak, we are the sewer rats,' Fay and the rest of the girls echoed.

Petra chuckled at Nat. 'Have you got a problem with the sewer rats, Nat? We are sneaky, resourceful, smart and know how to look after ourselves.'

Nat grinned. 'And you all smell like them, too.'

'Hey,' Harriet said, jumping into Nat's arms. 'You stink too.'

Petra, Nat and Harold laughed at the wriggling Harriet.

'Yes, I suppose we all stink a little, don't we?' Petra said. 'I think it's time we get to work.'

'This place has hardly any light,' Nat said.

Harold walked along the wall until he found a decayed old torch. The wood crumbled in his hand but stayed mostly in one piece. He ripped a piece of his shirt and wrapped it around the torch. With a single strike of a match, he lit it. The flames danced.

'Oh wow,' Petra said. 'This place is bigger than I thought.'

'I think this was the central hub of the old town's sewers,' Harold said. 'We need to replace the torches and bring down supplies.'

'When do we start?' Petra said.

'We stay the night. In the morning, Nat and I will go up with some sewer rats and see what we can do,' Harold said, winking.

'Squeak, squeak,' Harriet said. 'I am a sewer rat.'

CHAPTER 7
MISTER H

Petra smiled at the girls standing to attention.

'Hold your short swords out in front of you,' Harold said, walking up and down the line. 'You must get used to the way it feels. How heavy it is, how the balance feels. It can one day save your life if you know how to use it properly.'

Fay jumped forward and swished her short sword.

'Back in line, Fay,' Harold said, the corners of his mouth turning up. 'Keep your line. Discipline is key.'

Fay pouted as she took a step back.

'Now, cut right, and left, and right again,' Harold said, swinging his sword.

The girls all swung their small swords in unison.

'Very well done. Now let's practise putting on our masks,' Harold said, reaching into his hood and clipping his mask into place. 'If they cannot see your face, they cannot blame you for anything.'

'I will just run away really fast, mister,' a young girl said as she struggled to put hers on.

Harold dropped to a knee. 'Running is really important. Hold the clip like this and click it like that.'

The young girl snapped the mask into place, then lifted her head. Harold smiled as he pulled the ill-fitting cotton hood tighter over her head.

'We need to get better material,' Nat said, sitting down next to Petra.

'You have done a good job with their new clothes,' Petra said. 'They will be hard to spot in the shadows.'

'It is a pity you haven't seen these girls in action,' Nat said. 'They are stealthy and hard to catch.'

'I bet Donte is very angry at not having any girls to catch,' Petra said, with a look of satisfaction.

'He is still searching for you,' Nat said. 'There has been no sign of your father. From what I hear, he is still in the City of Lynn.'

'I hope he stays there,' Petra said. 'I don't want him having to deal with Donte.'

'Jump,' Harold shouted. 'Jump, and jump,' he said again. 'Well done. Keep going.'

Petra took in a sharp breath.

'Are you OK?' Nat said, placing a hand on her shoulder.

'Just a few sharp pains,' Petra said. 'They go away quickly.'

'I wish we could get you up to a doctor,' Nat said. 'We should have you checked out.'

'You know that will never happen,' Petra said. 'Like you said, Donte is still looking for me.'

'We can always get a doctor down here,' Nat said. 'Leonard said he can get that organised.'

Petra placed both hands on her belly and sat back against the wall. 'I am fine, Nat. I need you to start preparing for the birth.'

'Yes, I am already,' Nat said, smiling. 'I have the supplies ready at my new home. I will bring them down this week.'

'No, no, no,' Harold said, kneeling in front of a girl. 'You hold it like this. That's it, well done.'

'Two more goes and then it's break time, Harold,' Petra said.

Harold smiled and gave her a nod.

The girls picked up their swords again and twirled around the big room, swishing left and right. The older ones stopped and helped the younger girls when they stumbled to the ground. After one more go around the room, they replaced their swords in the holders and sat cross-legged, breathing hard.

'You have all done very well,' Harold said, his face full of pride. 'We will practise every day until we become the best.'

The girls all clapped.

'Ow,' Petra said, doubling over.

'Something is wrong, Petra,' Nat said nervously. 'We need to get someone to look at you.'

'We cannot trust anyone,' Petra said, taking in deep breaths. 'The pain is going already. I am OK.'

'You are one month too early,' Harold said, sitting on a ledge. 'You should not be feeling any pain. I think we should ask Leonard to send the doctor.'

'I will be fine,' Petra said. 'Help me get to the blankets and let me lie down.'

Nat and Harold helped her into the blankets, where she stretched out on her side.

'Comfortable?' Nat said.

Petra nodded. 'I will be fine.'

'Mr Harold, can we practise our jumps?' a girl said.

Harold turned his worried eyes off Petra and smiled at the girl. 'We can practise, but I think it's time we make it a little harder. What do you think?'

'Yes,' the girls said, clapping their hands. 'What are we going to do, Mister H?'

'That's a new one,' Harold said, smiling at Petra. 'I have never been called Mr H.'

'It suits you,' Petra said, smiling. 'So, Mr H, how are you going to make it more difficult for these young sewer rats?'

Harold walked to the back of the room and picked up a thin plank. He placed each end of the plank on opposite ledges.

'We can walk over the plank, Mr H,' Fay said.

'But can you run and jump?' Harold said as he picked up a bucket of dirty water and then placed it in the middle of the plank. 'Come on. Line up.'

The young girls scrambled into a line at the side of the ledge. One by one, they jumped over the dirty bucket of water.

'Very good,' Harold said. 'Well done. Now again, but much faster.'

'Harold,' Petra said, sucking air through her teeth. 'Harold, Nat, help me.'

Harold took three large strides and knelt next to his granddaughter. 'What is it?'

'Something is wrong with the baby,' Petra said, her eyes wide. 'I think I am going to have it now.'

'It's too early,' Nat said, her hand snaking under Petra's head.

Petra cried out.

'This is bad,' Nat said. 'This is very bad.'

'Help me, Nat,' Petra said, her teeth grinding together.

'Quick, get me blankets,' Nat shouted to the girls.

Petra's head lolled from side to side. 'So much pain,' she hissed. 'I am going to throw up.'

'Harold, spread this out over her,' Nat said.

Petra felt Harold's strong hands pick her up. She felt herself starting to lose consciousness. She shook her head to bring back the light, but the darkness took her.

'Is she OK, miss?' Harriet said.

'She will be now,' Nat said.

Petra shook her head. 'What happened?'

'You passed out,' Nat said.

'The baby,' Petra said. 'Where is my baby?'

Nat dabbed Petra's head.

'Where is my baby, Nat?' Petra shouted.

'She is with the doctor.'

Petra's head snapped to the right. 'Hargreaves,' she hissed. 'What have you done with my baby?'

Hargreaves knelt next to Petra. 'You passed out. Fay came to get me. She told me something was wrong.'

'Did I do the wrong thing, miss?' Fay said.

'Where is my baby?' Petra said, reaching out and grabbing Hargreaves by the collar.

He took her hand. 'She is with a doctor. She is safe, Petra. You need to trust me.'

'Trust you?' Petra shouted. 'Why would I trust you? Bring back my baby right now.'

'She is safe, Petra,' Hargreaves said, a tear spilling down his cheek. 'I am sorry I walked away from you and our baby. I am so sorry.'

'I don't care what you did,' Petra said. 'Give me back my baby.'

'My lady,' Harold said, kneeling on the other side of Petra. 'Your little one wasn't breathing. We had to give her to the doctor to make sure she survived.'

Petra pulled her hand away from Hargreaves and grabbed Harold's hand. 'It's a she? Is she going to be OK?'

'It's a little girl,' Harold said. 'And I think she will be OK. The doctor needs to keep her safe for a bit.'

'I want to see her,' Petra said, struggling to sit.

'Lie still,' Nat said, pressing down on Petra's chest. 'We had to cut the baby out and you have stitches.'

'I want to see my baby, Nat,' Petra said, her eyes frantically darting from Nat to Harold.

'Look at me, Petra,' Hargreaves said. 'I have organised somewhere for you to go. Somewhere for you to go with our child. Somewhere both of you may have a chance of a normal life.'

'What are you talking about, Hargreaves?' Petra said.

'Our child cannot come down here into the sewers,' Hargreaves said. 'She is too weak, and the sewers are no place to raise a child.'

'You didn't have a problem with these little girls living in the alleys,' Nat said, her lip curling. 'Nor do you have a problem with them living in the sewers.'

Hargreaves held up a hand. 'I know what it looks like and I know I should have done something about that.'

'Where is this place?' Harold said.

'South, above the cliffs,' Hargreaves said. 'There are schools who need teachers. I have a relative who will take Petra in.'

'My family is here, Hargreaves,' Petra said. 'I want my baby here with me and her great-grandfather.'

'My lady, I think we should listen,' Harold said. 'I would like my granddaughter and great-granddaughter to be safe.'

'Listen to your grandpapa, Petra. They are schools for girls. Men are not allowed to visit. You and our baby will be safe. Donte will not find you there,' Hargreaves said.

Petra dropped her head into the blankets. 'I don't want to leave my family behind.'

'Your baby is your family,' Harold said. 'And Nat can always visit.'

Hargreaves opened his mouth, then slammed it shut as Nat's elbow found his ribs.

A few moments later, Petra opened her eyes and looked at Harold. 'Do you promise to bring my baby to me?'

'I will bring the little one to you,' Harold said. 'This I will promise you. With my life.'

Petra reached up and touched his face. 'I do love you, Grandpapa.'

Harold cleared his throat. He took Petra's hand and kissed her knuckles. 'I love you too, little one.'

'How do I get to this school?' Petra said, looking at Hargreaves.

Hargreaves dropped back onto his heels. He closed his eyes and sighed. 'You have to travel through the wheat fields, up the valley and through the cliff forests. It is not a simple journey.'

'How do we expect Petra to do that in her state?' Nat said.

'She will have help,' Hargreaves said, looking at Nat. 'Peter will take her.'

Nat placed a hand on her mouth. 'Peter is alive? Everyone told me they had killed him.'

'He is in hiding,' Hargreaves said. 'Ever since Donte forced us to make the moustached man the captain of Fairacre, he has been hunting Peter.'

'What about Petra?' Harold said. 'She has stitches and can hardly move.'

'The doctor said she could move in a few days,' Hargreaves said. 'I suggest you rest, Petra. You need to prepare yourself for the journey.'

Petra closed her eyes and took in a deep breath. 'If I get to see my baby, no journey will be too big.'

Hargreaves let out a long sigh.

'Miss,' Fay said, kneeling at Petra's feet. 'I saw your baby. She looks lovely.'

Petra smiled at Fay. 'Did you really see her?'

'Yes, miss,' Fay said. 'The doctor said she will be OK.'

'Thank you, Fay,' Petra said as she reached over and then squeezed her hand.

'Are you going to give her a name, miss?' Harriet said.

'Juno,' Petra said. 'One day she will be the protector of women, therefore I will name her Juno.'

'Juno,' Harriet said, clapping her hands.

'Are you sure you are ready for this?' Harold said, checking Petra's small pack.

'Yes, Grandpapa,' she said, pulling the bag tighter to her back. 'I feel strong.'

'Here is some extra food,' Nat said, slipping a small package into the top of her pack. 'You be safe now.'

Petra pulled Nat into a hug. 'I love you, my dearest friend.'

'I love you too,' Nat mumbled into her shoulder.

'I want the two of you to promise me something,' Petra said, looking at Harold and Nat.

'Anything,' Nat said.

'I need you to keep the sewer rats safe. I need you to train them and make them strong.'

Harold smiled. 'I will make sure I train them well, my lady.'

'Everyone,' Hargreaves said. 'I need you all to listen to me very carefully.'

Harold and Nat stopped fussing with Petra's backpack. Petra and Peter turned to face Hargreaves.

'From today, it will not be Petra they will remember as the creator of the sewer rats,' Hargreaves said. 'From today, it will be

Harold and Nat. Nobody can ever say Petra's name again. It is too unsafe. Are we clear on this?'

Harold, Nat and Peter nodded.

'I don't care who founded the sewer rats,' Petra said. 'All I want is for them to be safe and happy.'

'It is time, my lady,' Peter said. 'The sun has set.'

Nat walked over to Peter and hugged him. 'Be safe and look after my friend, will you?'

Petra hugged Harold and Nat one more time. She walked over to Hargreaves and hugged him. 'Look after Juno and bring her back to me.'

'Let's go,' Peter said.

They walked out of the metal door and down through the sewers. After a number of turns, they reached a small gate. Peter pulled the chain off and opened it. Petra walked through, crouched and looked up at the moon. As they turned south, Petra looked to the east at the walls of her home town, Fairacre.

'We move through wheat fields and into the valley,' Peter whispered. 'Stay very close to me.'

Petra kept her head low as they moved silently through the wheat fields. Peter moved slowly to accommodate Petra's healing belly. The wheat swished in the gentle breeze.

'Miss,' a girl whispered.

Peter knelt and gently pulled Petra down with him. 'Did you hear that?' he said.

'Yes,' Petra said, turning her head from side to side. 'I don't know where it came from.'

'Me neither,' Peter said as he scanned the top of the wheat.

'Boo,' Harriet said, jumping out of the wheat with her arms in the air. 'I found you, miss.'

Petra grabbed Harriet and pulled her into a hug. 'What are you doing here, you silly girl?'

Harriet pulled away and pouted. 'I am playing hide and seek, like in the sewers.'

'Well, you certainly found us,' Peter said. 'Now what?'

'We should take her back,' Petra said.

Peter lifted his head above the wheat and looked the way they had come. 'If we go back, we cannot go to the cliffs tonight. We need to go another time.'

'I don't want to go back to the sewers,' Harriet said, folding her arms. 'I want to come with you, Miss Petra.'

Petra thought for a moment, then looked at Peter. 'Do you think we can manage with Harriet?'

'If there is any trouble along the way, we will struggle,' Peter said. 'If it's clear, then yes, we can manage with little Harriet.'

'So, young lady,' Petra said. 'It looks like you can come, but it's to a brand-new world.'

Harriet clapped.

Petra grabbed the young girl's hands. 'Shh, we need to move quietly. There are bad men looking for us.'

'Will they hurt us?' Harriet whispered. 'Like the snatchers?'

'Yes, they will hurt us. It is the same people, so you need to be extra quiet, OK?'

Harriet placed a finger on her lips. 'I will be extra quiet.'

'Good,' Petra said. 'Now follow close behind Peter and I will be behind you.'

Peter continued towards the southern treeline. The trees climbed high up into the air. When they stopped walking, they could hear the distant thunder of water crashing into a body of water. Half an hour later, they stepped out of the wheat field and into the forest.

'We have a long way to go,' Peter said, picking up the pace.

Harriet skipped forward and pointed up the valley. 'Are we going all the way up there?'

'Yes, we are,' Peter said, smiling. 'We go up the valley, then through the forest to the village.'

'Don't go too far forward,' Petra called after Harriet. 'We cannot see you too well in the dark.'

'Will they accept her at the school?' Peter said.

'I will make them accept her,' Petra said. 'It is a school for girls, isn't it?'

Peter suddenly stopped. He lifted his head and sniffed.

'What is it?' Petra whispered.

'We are being followed,' Peter said. 'Get Harriet back here.'

'Harriet,' Petra said. 'Where are you?'

'There is something wrong,' Peter said. 'It's too quiet.'

A long, low howl sounded from further up the valley.

'What is that?' Petra said.

'Wolves,' Peter said. 'We need to keep moving.'

'Harriet,' Petra shouted. 'Get back here.'

Harriet jumped out from behind a rock and ran over. 'I am sorry, Miss Petra. Please don't shout.'

'Let's keep moving,' Peter said. 'Stay quiet and stay together.'

They continued up the path. Fallen logs and hidden stones made them occasionally trip.

'I can hear them,' Harriet whispered. 'I can hear the snatchers.'

'Keep going,' Petra said. 'We need to speed up.'

The howls of the wolves grew nearer.

'What is that noise?' Harriet said.

'Wolves,' Peter said. 'Like big dogs.'

Harriet looked back at Petra with wide eyes.

An hour later, the sounds of guards' feet crunching on the fallen leaves reached their ears.

'How much further?' Petra said.

'We are nearly at the top,' Peter said. 'Once we get there, we turn left and walk along the cliff edge until we reach the river. Follow the river up to the village.'

'I can hear them up the valley,' a man shouted.

'They have found us,' Peter said. 'We have to move quickly.'

'Take Harriet,' Peter said. 'If I tell you to run, you run.'

They continued onwards. Peter stopped every few minutes and checked behind them. Men's voices trickled up the valley.

'They will soon be on us,' Peter said.

A howl sounded from near the valley's top.

A few minutes later, Peter brought them to a halt. He looked down then up the valley. 'I will have to leave you,' he said, facing Petra.

'Where are you going?' Harriet said.

Peter pulled Petra and Harriet into a hug. 'If you see Nat, please tell her I love her.'

'What are you going to do?' Petra said. 'Don't leave us here, Peter.'

'You,' a man shouted.

Petra grabbed Harriet and spun around. Peter spun and drew his sword.

The captain with his massive moustache pointed a sword at them. 'Donte wants you home where you belong.'

'I am not going anywhere,' Petra said. 'Tell him he cannot have me.'

The captain marched up the valley. Four guards followed behind.

'Run,' Peter shouted, before charging at the captain.

Petra turned to run but stopped in her tracks. A large black wolf stood on a rock above them. The sound of steel hitting steel echoed through the valley.

'I don't want any trouble,' Petra said, holding out a hand.

'Good doggie,' Harriet said.

The wolf tilted his head and sniffed the air. Another grey wolf jumped onto the rock and stared at them.

A scream sounded from behind Petra. She spun around to see Peter pulling his sword out of a guard. The captain ignored Peter and marched towards Petra.

'Leave us alone,' Petra shouted.

The captain pointed his sword at her. 'Come home or I will end that child's life.'

Petra took a step back. The captain continued up the path. The whooshing sound of a sword swirling through the air spun the captain around. The point of Peter's flying sword stabbed him in the shoulder. The captain fell to a knee.

'Run,' Peter screamed.

Petra turned just in time to see a guard stab Peter in the chest.

'Peter,' Petra screamed.

Harriet burst into tears.

Petra turned and walked as fast as she could up the hill. The wolves watched her pass.

'Get back here,' the captain shouted. 'Guards, get her.'

'The snatchers are coming,' Harriet said.

Suddenly, a stream of wolves sprang out of the trees. Behind her, Petra heard the screams of men and the howls of wolves. She reached the top of the cliff and turned left.

'The wolves are fighting the snatchers,' Harriet said.

'Can you run next to me, Harriet?' Petra said.

Harriet struggled out of Petra's grasp and landed on the ground. She started running along the cliff edge.

'I can hear the water,' Harriet said. 'I think it is over there.'

They reached a large willow. A dark stream of water surged past the tree and over the cliff.

'We go south now and follow the river,' Petra said.

They continued until they found a tree trunk across the river.

Harriet ran across like it was a plank over an alley. Petra held out her arms and walked over slowly.

'I can hear the snatchers,' Harriet whispered. 'They are near the waterfall.'

Petra hurried forward through the forest. A single path wound around the tree trunks. Half an hour later, they burst out of the trees and ran past a small well. Up a cobblestone path, Petra saw the village lights.

'They are coming,' Harriet said, grabbing Petra's hand. 'We need to run, Miss Petra.'

Petra placed her hand on her belly and felt a warm, wet patch. She looked at her hand and saw it covered in an oily liquid.

'Are you OK, Miss?' Harriet said.

'I am bleeding, Harriet,' Petra said, dropping to a knee.

'We need to go, miss,' Harriet said, pulling Petra's hand.

Petra struggled to her feet and walked towards the village. The lights of the little cottages grew bigger and bigger.

'We are nearly there,' Harriet said.

'I can't go any longer,' Petra said, dropping to her knees. 'Run, Harriet. Find the school.'

CHAPTER 8
YOU CANNOT TELL ANYONE

Petra slowly opened her eyes.

'Miss Petra,' Harriet said. 'You are awake.'

'Where are we?' Petra said, wincing from the pain in her side.

'We are at the school,' Harriet said. 'I will get the teacher.'

Petra watched Harriet disappear out of the door. A few minutes later, a tall slender woman with an aquiline nose walked into the room.

'You see,' Harriet said, pointing at Petra. 'I told you she was awake.'

'Well done, now fetch me some water, will you?' the woman said.

'Yes, miss,' Harriet said, disappearing down the corridor.

'Well, well,' the slender woman said, as she pulled up a chair. 'I never thought I would see you wake up. You are very lucky.'

'What happened?' Petra said.

'Young Harriet nearly broke down every door in the village,' the woman said. 'A kindly gentleman brought you to us here at the school.'

Petra pushed herself up. She winced from the aches and stabbing pains coursing through her body.

'You shouldn't move too much,' the woman said. 'We have had to stitch you up again.'

'Who are you?' Petra said.

'I am Edith, Hargreaves's aunt,' she said. 'I am the principal of this school.'

'Hargreaves told you I was coming?' Petra said.

'He did, but he didn't tell me you were being chased.'

Petra stared at her. 'Donte. Did he find me?'

Edith's lip curled. 'A man with a moustache came looking, but he didn't enter the grounds of our school. The City of Lynn forbids it.'

With a long sigh, Petra leant back into her pillow. 'So Harriet is safe? I am safe?'

'You are both safe,' Edith said, patting Petra on the forearm. 'I have Harriet enrolled in school already.'

'That is great news,' Petra said. 'Any news from Hargreaves?'

Edith shook her head. 'He will play it low. I doubt we will hear from him for a long while.'

A tear ran down Petra's face.

'He will keep his promise,' Edith said. 'He will return your baby to you. You just have to be patient.'

'Here we go, miss,' Harriet said, entering the room with some water.

'Thank you, Harriet,' Petra said, taking the glass and having a sip.

'We need to let Petra rest,' Edith said. 'We can visit her tomorrow.'

'OK, miss,' Harriet said as she leant over and then hugged Petra.

Edith and Harriet left the room. Petra closed her eyes and went to sleep.

'Be careful,' Edith said. 'Don't tear those stitches.'

Petra sat up in bed then swung her feet over the edge. She tentatively stood up while holding onto Edith. Her body ached with pain.

'We are going to do a small walk,' Edith said. 'Then I have something for you.'

They left the room and walked up a long corridor. Petra smiled at the sounds of the girls in the distance.

'You can do it, miss,' Harriet said, running past them. 'You be careful, miss.'

'Get back to your class,' Edith shouted. 'Go on, get back.'

'Yes, miss,' Harriet said, running out of the hallway.

Edith turned Petra around and walked her back to her room. 'We will be doing that once a day from now on.'

Petra gave Edith a weak smile. 'Thank you so much.'

'Get back into bed,' Edith said. 'I have something for you.'

The bed squeaked as Petra climbed into it. She pulled the covers up to her waist. Edith passed her a small white envelope.

'I will leave you to it,' Edith said, walking over to the door. 'Ring the bell if you need me.'

Petra waited for the door to close. She grabbed the corner of the envelope and ripped.

Petra.

I have cleared the way for our baby Juno. I will leave her by the river tonight.

H.

. . .

Petra grabbed the bell and frantically rang it.

A girl opened the door. 'Can I help you, miss?'

'Can you get Edith immediately for me, please?'

'Yes, miss,' the girl said, closing the door.

Petra placed her head back on the pillow. 'Come on. Come on,' she said.

'What is bothering you?' Edith said.

'Sorry to be so urgent, but when did you get this letter?'

'We got it this morning,' Edith said.

'And what time is it now?' Petra said.

'Nearly dinner time. Is there something wrong?'

Petra handed Edith the letter.

'Oh my,' Edith said, walking out of the door. 'Wait here, please.'

'I am not waiting,' Petra said, climbing out of bed and walking out. She made her way along the hallway until she reached the door at the end. Petra opened the door and stepped out into a large corridor with arches running the length of it. The sound of girls came from the right. She followed the chattering until she walked through a door into a massive dining hall. The chatter stopped and hundreds of girls stared at her.

'Miss Petra,' Harriet said, jumping off her bench. 'You should be in bed.'

'Where is the river, Harriet?' Petra said.

'I will get into trouble, miss,' Harriet said, looking down at her hands.

'You won't get into trouble,' Petra said. 'I will make sure of it.'

'OK, miss,' Harriet said. 'Follow me.'

Petra followed Harriet through the dining hall and into the next corridor. They walked down it until they came to a glass double door. Harriet swung open the doors and walked into the greenhouse.

'What is this place?' Petra said, as they walked through the big glass room.

'We grow food and plants,' Harriet said. 'I have a class here every day.'

They continued through the greenhouse until they reached the doors to the outside.

'The river is down there,' Harriet said, pointing down the green.

Petra put her hand over her eyes. In the distance, Edith bent over and picked something up off the ground.

'Juno,' Petra whispered.

Harriet grabbed Petra's hand. 'Is that your baby?'

Petra smiled at Harriet. 'We will see.'

Edith strode back towards them.

'Here she comes, miss,' Harriet said.

Petra placed her hand on her forehead and looked past Edith. In the distance, a large lone man waved. Petra lifted her hand and gave a single wave. 'Is it Juno?' Petra said, as Edith came closer.

'It is,' Edith said with a wide smile. 'A beautiful baby girl.'

Petra held out her arms.

Edith handed Juno to her.

Tears streaked down Petra's face. Young Juno looked up at her and gurgled.

'Let's get you back to your room,' Edith said. 'Harriet, I need you to come too.'

'OK, miss,' Harriet said as she jumped, trying to get a view of Juno.

Edith led them through some back corridors until they reached the teachers' quarters. They walked down the corridor and into Petra's room.

'Sit, please,' Edith said.

Petra sat on her bed and Harriet sat next to her.

Edith sat on the chair. 'You both need to listen to me very carefully.'

'Is something wrong, miss?' Harriet said.

'Nothing is wrong,' Edith said. 'But I have something important to tell you.'

Petra and Harriet both nodded.

'You cannot tell anyone Juno is your daughter,' Edith said. 'She needs to believe she is an orphan. Left down by the river.'

'But Petra is her mother,' Harriet said.

'I know,' Edith said. 'But if someone finds out Petra is Juno's mother, they might want to hurt Juno.'

'Donte,' Petra said. 'He will try to hurt her.'

'He will,' Edith said. 'So you cannot claim her as your daughter.'

'I understand,' Petra said.

'Do you understand, Harriet?' Edith said.

Harriet nodded.

'But I want you to promise me one thing, Harriet,' Petra said.

'What, miss?' Harriet said.

'I need you to always look out for little Juno,' Petra said. 'Can you promise me that?'

Harriet leant over and kissed Juno on the forehead. 'I promise, miss.'

'Let's leave Petra and Juno alone, shall we, Harriet?' Edith said.

'OK, miss,' Harriet said, leaving the room.

'Are you going to be OK?' Edith said.

Petra looked up at Edith. 'Now that Juno is here, I have never been happier.'

CHAPTER 9
EPILOGUE

A day later.

'Is it done?'

'It's done,' Harold said. 'Petra has Juno in her arms.'

'That is wonderful news,' Hargreaves said. 'It looks like Donte has given up the search for now.'

'Will she be safe there?' Harold said.

'It's the safest place to be,' Hargreaves said.

A week later.

'How is Nat?' Hargreaves said.

'She is heartbroken,' Harold said. 'We finally found Peter's body.'

'I spoke to the captain about it,' Hargreaves said. 'He claims he knows nothing about it.'

'Looks like he died at the hands of the Fairacre guards,' Harold said. 'There are tell-tale wounds.'

'I have no idea how that happened,' Hargreaves said. 'The captain says he will investigate.'

'Any news on Ernest?' Harold said.

'I sent him a letter,' Hargreaves said. 'He replied, saying he was going to stay in the City of Lynn. He has asked me to move into his house in the northern district.'

'If you need anything,' Harold said, 'get hold of me through a messenger. I am permanently with the sewer rats now.'

Hargreaves nodded. 'Have a good day, Harold.'

'And you,' Harold said, disappearing into an alley.

A month later

'Psst,' Fay said. 'What's your name?'

'Who's asking?' the girl said.

'How long have you been living in the alleys?' Fay said. 'I used to live in the alleys.'

The girl frowned. 'Where do you live now?'

'Tell me what your name is,' Fay said.

The girl looked up and down the alley. 'My name is Naomi.'

'Hi, Naomi,' Fay said. 'My name is Fay.'

'Hi, Fay,' Naomi said.

'So tell me, Naomi,' Fay said, 'have you ever heard of the sewer rats?'

NEXT UP...

Juno and the Lady (The Acre Series Book 1)

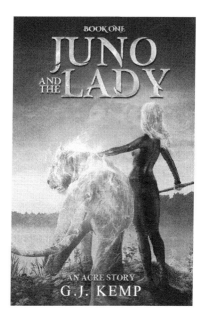

Juno's beloved Petra is dead.

Petra's replacement, the mysterious Lady, has put Juno's best friend Tilly
under a dark spell that has left Juno with nobody she can trust.

With only Chax, her kitten, for company, Juno escapes from her school to
a town at the bottom of the cliffs.

A town ruled by men.

Alone, scared, and without friends, Juno feels an unknown power growing inside her. A power she knows she will one day have to harness. With all lost, a dark figure from within the shadows cups her mouth and whispers in her ear to keep quiet.

Juno joins her new friends but just as she starts to learn how the world really works, the ill-tempered Dr Viktor demands an audience.

Juno and the Lady is a young woman's journey into a land of the old ways, where men rule, and women are property.

With unlikely friendships, forbidden love and burning magic, can Juno change the conventions of old? Can she save the town? And will she figure out who the Lady truly is?

AUTHOR REQUEST

Hello,

Thank you for taking the time to read **Petra and the Sewer Rats**. It is the second prequel novella of Juno and the Lady. I will be releasing more Juno novellas in the months to come.

If you have a moment, I would really appreciate a review on either Amazon or Goodreads. The reviews help us indie authors a great deal.

Please consider joining my mailing list where I will keep you up to date with book release dates, news and upcoming events. https://gjkemp.co.uk/mailing-list/

Again, thank you for spending your precious time reading my books.

Take care,
G.J.

ABOUT THE AUTHOR

A nomad at heart, GJ has lived in nine countries across Africa, Europe and the Middle East. His career has included working as a Divemaster in The Red Sea, a zookeeper in Israel, and a proof-reader in Sweden. Born with cerebral palsy, GJ has spent a lifetime trying to tie his shoelaces while standing up in the hope of not falling over. It is a constant challenge, but sometimes he occasionally succeeds.

Finding the love for writing later in life, GJ spends most of his free time going for walks and dreaming of story ideas. He hopes to one day have a small place on the oceanfront where he can walk his dogs on the beach.

For more information please visit gjkemp.co.uk

facebook.com/gavin.kemp.92505
twitter.com/TB5Publishing
instagram.com/tb5publishing
linkedin.com/in/g-j-kemp-4a76b03
bookbub.com/profile/g-j-kemp

Printed in Great Britain
by Amazon